Night Riders
in the Tallgrass

Night Riders
in the **Tallgrass**

Mo Griffin

Night Riders in the Tallgrass

Published by Wheatmark®
1760 East River Road, Suite 145
Tucson, Arizona 85718 U.S.A.
www.wheatmark.com

ISBN: 978-1-60494-835-6
LCCN: 2013930062

For my wife, Tula, for her many gifts of historical references, encouragement, and love.

Not for the glory of winning;
Not for the fear of the night;
Shunning the battle is sinning;
Oh spare me the heart to fight!

"Battle Cry" by John G. Neihardt

Acknowledgments

My deepest thanks go out to my son Timothy, a gifted writer, for his guidance, support, and tolerance. Sincere gratitude is also owed to those who live and experience the tallgrass prairie on a regular basis. For decades these friends have shared their love of the land and unique stories and knowledge. I have walked and ridden with them in these spaces. This tale could never have been possible without those invaluable times we shared.

To Kat Gautreaux, many thanks for her timely professional guidance throughout the development of this book. Thanks also to Susan Wenger for her creative designs and valuable input.

Finally, none of this would have transpired without the love and patience of my wife, Tula.

Prologue

It was June of 1861, while a member of Ben McCulloch's band of eight hundred, when the famous ranger had noticed a quiet and deadly sharpshooter with the name of Ty McCord. Ty was sixteen years old and the son of Irish immigrants. None of his famous troop knew where he hailed from—and he offered no clue. The loose-knit raiders from Texas had crossed the northern border of Arkansas, swiftly advancing toward Springfield, Missouri, where they would confront a larger but untried Union force. The confrontation would prove to be the final pitched battle that young McCord would fight in the Civil War. However, it was in the hills and woods of southwestern Missouri where he proved McCulloch's instincts had been right as rain. The first general to die in the Civil War, Nathan Lyon, fell before the young marksman. It was said the strapping raider killed fourteen Union officers. In less than twenty-four hours, McCulloch's men withdrew without pursuit, taking Ty McCord and his raiders back the way they had come. Later that same month, they disbanded and scattered to the winds.

Back in Arkansas, on June 30, 1861, that same boy shot a hanging rope from my neck as I was preparing to meet my Maker. Three drunken ruffians sent by the devil died that grim day, making it possible for me to preach the word of our Lord and Savior.

The diary of Reverend Reyfus A. Williams, Pastor Calvary Baptist Church, Cedarville, Arkansas, June 1, 1862. Neotris Green Williams, widow of the Reverend Williams, noted the two men often sent notes and letters through friends until the death of Reverend Williams, December 26, 1888.

(Blessed Archives of Calvary Baptist Church)

Part One
Destination Tallgrass

Ben and Grey

It was the years after the war that he was mulling over now; his days as a ranger in Lubbock and Amarillo, along with Laredo, had been rough, and he had seen the good and evil in many men—and some women, too. The worst of the lot and their violent natures often had caused an early death for innocent citizens. With his ranger days behind him, Ty was different. The loss of his only true love to a good man of means in Laredo had finally sent him drifting on a long, sandy, dusty trail through northwest Texas, on to Masterson, then north to Cactus and eventually landing him in Guymon, Oklahoma. It was the home of his old friend, Captain Ben McCulloch. From there, the trail would take him across the Cimarron River and eventually into the flatlands of the Kansas prairie, where he had ventured in his lawman past.

In Guymon, Ty found Ben in fine spirits for a man of seventy-seven. Ben had served quite a few years as sheriff, before finally retiring—if a man could call running the town's stables a fitting retirement. Two days of rest with good conversation had set Ty back on the trail fit and full of the latest gossip. Upon departing, Ty had said his good-byes, returning to the stables only to discover his little roan missing. In her place was the most magnificent gray stallion he had ever laid eyes on. The monster stood every bit of sixteen hands, showing strong, powerful haunches with a regal, huge, and perfectly shaped head. He was beautiful, with a blue-gray angular marking running from his wide nostrils to his broad forehead. Dark stockings set off his long powerful legs. He was the lone gift Ty had received in his lifetime, unless a man counted the .44 Colt revolver and Winchester rifle issued to him when he had joined the rangers after the war. He would have to find a way somehow to repay the Captain.

In a few short hours, the gray brute was eating miles as they crossed the Cimarron, moving northeast toward Dodge City—all the while suspicious of his easy-riding stranger. The power of the animal surged through Ty's muscular six-foot-three frame. Eventually, sparse flatland began to give way to small, barren hills and occasional shallow streams, rivulets, and slews. Most contained water. Presently, large expanses of grass showed here and there, and he passed two far-off farms barely seen in the distance. Grey flew by them all on this first of September. As was his nature, Ty had a well-thought-out plan. They would reach Dodge on the third day, barring the unexpected. Two nights under the stars with the prairie winds would suit Ty just fine. The way the beast was covering the trail, perhaps Dodge would come into view sooner than Ty had planned. The dried beef strips, beans, and coffee in his saddlebags were more than adequate to see them through to Dodge. Grey would get his daily ration of sugar, too.

As the first day rolled on, Ty's thoughts returned to his days in Laredo. He remembered fondly the only woman he had truly wanted. Shy and gentle was her way. His life as a ranger didn't fit her idea of a future, so Ed Turnbull had stolen her fair and square. Ed was a good man and a solid citizen—a man Ty couldn't hate. She had wanted more than Ty could have given her, despite the fact he had helped save her life when she found herself in the midst of a botched bank robbery. Since that bloody event, buckshot was occasionally working its way through Ty's skin, serving as a constant reminder of their last days together—his full-fledged best days for certain. Ty rode on with his hurt, and Grey continued consuming mile after mile of the narrow prairie trail until the late evening. It was only then that Ty remembered the thousand dollars in banknotes concealed in his bedroll. Ben had given him the money to add to his own four hundred dollars for a substantial down payment should he find his own place in the tallgrass country—yet another debt to old Ben.

By sundown, Grey had found adequate grass and water in a nearby sliver of a creek. A generous helping of beans and dried beef, along with hot coffee, sat just right for Ty. The sun had disappeared from the western sky. With his saddle behind his head and his Winchester rifle by his side, Ty soon drifted off. He wondered if he was becoming a hopeless, lonely saddle tramp.

The Simmonses

Steaming black coffee with some biscuits did the trick for Ty, as they always had. Minutes before sunup, as was his habit, Ty mounted Grey, and the two galloped back on the trail. The sure-footed brute seemed more comfortable with his rider now, as he splashed through a knee-deep stream and up a jagged rocky bank and then skirted several buffalo wallows, pounding onto a wider trail, made so by the hundreds of hard men moving massive herds of cattle up from Texas and Oklahoma to the Kansas railheads. More often than not, the ranchers and their valuable cattle had to deal with fire, lightning, stampedes, rustlers, and, occasionally, marauding Indian braves. It was dangerous, brutal work. The famous Blacket outfit, along with the huge Goodnight bunch as well as many smaller ranchers just kept on coming. Ty remembered fondly a good number of them he had met and worked with. Most of the rough-hewn drovers, a man could depend on—unless you were a horse trader or bad with a deck of cards.

The high-spirited stallion and Ty rode on through a landscape of little hills and broad expanses of prairie. Sound carried forever in this land, but all Ty could really hear was the constant rhythm of Grey's hooves. He liked it this way, trusting himself and Grey. Stopping now and then for water and something from his well-worn saddlebags, they moved steadily on until early evening, having covered more ground in one day than he could ever remember. Finally, he reined in along a small creek flowing with clear, cold water; no doubt it came from a nearby spring. A lone cottonwood leaned gracefully over the stream. He hung his saddle blanket on it. Grey drank greedily and shivered with delight while Ty stripped to his underwear and waded into the waist-deep pool. The prairie winds would dry his clothes that he carefully hung on the tree. He felt good. Several green toads bounced along the bank while he wrung out more of his clothes. Grey had moved a dozen yards away, grazing in a stand of undersized grass.

In the distance, huge, black thunderheads were gathering in the pink-blue sky of the fading sun. Long, jagged lightning bolts slashed down through them. Ty could not hear the thunder; this storm could be a hundred miles from them. Ty seemed certain the weather was moving toward the north, and it would not bother them. Years in the open had been his lot for two decades, giving him a good sense of the prairie and flatland storms. If rain did come, it would not disturb his rest. Soon his little fire served up fresh coffee. Ben's jerky was seasoned and tasty. The hot pan of beans was followed with a long cheroot. There was just enough of a southwest breeze to keep the flying critters at bay, along with the smoke from his fire that streamed into the wind, while he pondered the endless expanse that lay ahead. He wondered how many hundreds of ragged, tired punchers had passed through the trail—some of them dying there. In two days, he had counted four graves, but how many were without a marker? For sure, many more were under the grass. Perhaps some had even been known to him as a younger man.

An hour before sunup, Ty was washing up in the stream. Rested and clear eyed, he grabbed his dry, wine-colored shirt off the cottonwood and tucked it in his pants. He then strapped on his Colt, slapping his Stetson before he put it on. A strong, cold wind was up, with the smell of rain in it. The night indeed had brewed yet another storm. A menacing sky was hanging low and close at hand, full of rain-filled black clouds; his morning coffee would have to wait. Nearby, a herd of leaping deer raced for shelter, and the morning birds were on the wing everywhere. Grey was anxious. Ty quickly saddled him and slipped the Winchester into its scabbard. Ty leaped into the saddle, giving the wild-eyed Grey the reins. He wanted to stay ahead of the building storm.

Later, a morning sun briefly joined them, highlighting the outline of a small house visible in the distance. It appeared there was cropland around with a fence in front of the house. Eventually, several horses appeared from behind the little home, where a well-built corral stood below a sizeable hillock; these folks no doubt were there to stay. As they advanced, Ty decided to stop. Grey had put them well ahead of the storm and deserved a rest. As they approached, a stocky, balding man stepped out onto his little porch. His suspenders were off his broad shoulders, and he was carrying a rifle. Ty reined in and slid from the saddle, keeping his eyes squarely on the homesteader.

"Good morning to you, sir," Ty offered. "I reckon you're fixing to get some rain. Looks like you've been getting some in recent days, by the looks of them creeks along the way."

The man examined Ty with care.

"I ain't seen a lone rider in a coon's age," he said as he extended his thick hand. His grip was strong. "You're a long way from nowhere, pardner. Sit yourself and take a load off. I see you've been riding in high style, judging by that fine stallion."

This was not a hard man. His round face and sparse, red hair were joined by deep-set, intelligent eyes and a small,

offset nose with a dent in its bridge. Ty seated himself in a
wooden chair and stretched his legs before him.

"I'm Darren Simmons. Coffee?" he offered, leaning his
rifle against the porch railing.

"I'd be much obliged. Ty McCord is my name. Pleased
to make your acquaintance."

"It's brewin' now. Won't be more than a minute or
two. Liz makes a damn fine pot, fit for a feller in need,"
he said. Both men looked toward the angry clouds in the
west.

Pushing his hat off his forehead, Ty inquired, "You set
your stakes here long?"

"Going on near five winters," Darren said proudly.
"Two of 'em was brewed by the devil hisself. The worst I
have ever seen. Killer storms. Done in all my livestock one
year, such as it was. Don't quite understand why I took to
this here land, really. Tornadoes with that damn, brutal,
constant wind ain't what most folks is hoping for in the
summer months."

Darren rose from his chair, disappearing inside the
little house. Ty noticed a prominent limp when he walked.
Seconds later, he returned to the porch with two tin
cups filled with thick, black coffee. "Liz's finest," Darren
announced, handing one cup to Ty. "You hungry? We
could feed a body some corn cakes, black beans. Don't
know a man ever disappointed by my daughter's cooking."

"Don't mind if I do," Ty said gratefully. "Me and Grey
got on the trail before sunup with no time to spare. We set
our minds to beat that storm. I'll admit I'm a mite hungry."

"We don't see many folks out here, Ty. Closest ones I
know is at least twenty-five miles to the east. Not too far
from a little town called Windville. Doc Crenshaw lives
there. Kept me alive when I got shot up on Tunnel Hill
in the Chattanooga campaign in '63. General Hooker got
four thousand of us wounded—and another seven hundred
killed—in four days. I was one of the lucky ones, sure as

hell. We come west together after the war. I'm glad to be among the walking. We both had our fill of them generals ... Hooker included. Johnny Reb and our boys from Virginia put no stock in killing each other. Had my fill of them yappy-mouthed politicians, too. Can't stand 'em, really." Ty savored his coffee and listened intently. "Say, cowboy, where you headed to anyway? Dodge?"

"That's my plan," Ty responded quietly.

Presently, Darren again disappeared inside. He returned with two large plates of hot food, with likely the prettiest woman Ty had ever laid eyes on. He tried not to stare at the auburn-haired girl, but he couldn't help himself. He jumped up and brushed his hair back. Reaching out, he carefully accepted the heaping, hot breakfast.

"This here is Ty McCord, Liz," Darren said with a wry smile.

"My pleasure, Liz," Ty managed to say.

"Well, then, sit yourself and clean that platter before it gets cold!" she ordered. Her large, green eyes sparkled when she spoke.

"Yes, ma'am," Ty answered as he lit into his food, using the best manners he could muster up. "Darren here said you really do yourself proud over a stove. I swear your corncakes are the best I ever put into my mouth. Beats the tar out of anything I ever tasted, for sure."

"Well, thank you," she acknowledged gratefully. "Father tells me you're on your way to Dodge. You have friends or family there?"

"Not that I know of. Just on my trail, more or less. A man can find a right decent bed in Dodge, I suppose," he answered, not revealing his ranger days that had taken him there in the past. Liz's straight-up way of speaking, all proper, made it clear to Ty that she had plenty of spirit along with book learnin'. She was also cocksure, knowing she was a sight to see.

The western thunderheads were suddenly pierced

again with jagged, long bolts of lightning, and loud, deep thunder rolled across the plains.

"Wish I could stay a little longer," Ty offered with regret. "But that thunder is a sign for me and Grey to get a move on. Can't thank you enough for the wonderful vittles, Miss Liz," he said as he handed her his plate. "I'm mighty grateful for sure. We should be on our way so we can stay ahead of that weather coming this way."

Darren and Liz traded quick glances as Ty started to step toward Grey.

"Wait a minute, there, son!" Darren shouted. "If you have no particular cause to ride on to Dodge except for a bed and a roof over your head, we'd be obliged to have you stay the night. You could put that monster of a horse in the barn. Besides, it's right unusual for a storm like that wicked-looking thing to brew itself up this early in the day. It looks downright nasty. If you aren't on a set time for a meeting situation, we'd like for you to stay. You may be glad to have a storm cellar nearby."

Ty didn't like the idea of losing a good half day, but one glance at Liz standing in the doorway was all a man needed to give in to the invite.

"Why, you're mighty nice, Darren, to offer. Yes, sir, you are, but I'll not accept unless I can help you out some way or another around your place."

"Then it's a deal," Darren said eagerly. "Turns out I could use a hand out back. Got a rock job around my well that needs a mite of finish work. This here bum leg is giving me fits recently."

In a half hour, Ty had slipped the saddle off the stallion, brushed him down, and seen to his water before leaving the barn. Grey watched with anxious eyes as Ty walked away toward the little house, trying to recall the last time he'd strayed from his intended schedule trail-wise. He was not a flexible man by nature, yet this change seemed right. Besides, the menacing storm was almost on them now.

The wind of the early morning was turning powerful and cold and oversized raindrops came down quickly, drenching him before he could reach the back door of the house.

Inside, Liz handed him more coffee. Wind whistled through the windows, followed by a deafening clap of thunder. Seconds later, ice rocks the size of chicken eggs assaulted the roof and began covering the drenched earth.

"This here's a dangerous one! That there lightning is dancing all around us. Looks like we're right in the storm's crosshairs," Darren blurted excitedly. "Better hurry to the storm cellar, Liz!"

Hiking her long, blue, gingham dress to her knees, Liz darted toward the shelter. Her long, auburn locks blew wild in the wind. Darren, behind her and completely soaked while being peppered with hailstones, skipped awkwardly as fast as he could until eventually disappearing down into the crude underground cellar.

Ty glanced skyward before madly dashing to the barn. Just then, the black sky ripped open, giving birth to a long, spiraling, half-mile-wide tornado that was flanked by two spike-shaped, miniature twisters. Ty ran diving into the confines of the small barn. Grey was snorting and wild with fear when Ty bolted into his stall. Ty gasped for air that the deadly tornado had sucked from his lungs. He couldn't hear himself breathe as he snapped a halter on Grey. He swiftly tied it to the center pole supporting Darren's structure. There was precious little air inside when suddenly half the roof disappeared into the violent, black sky full of flying debris.

Seconds later, the killer tornado receded into the boiling clouds that enveloped the endless prairie. Stepping outside, Ty noticed all four of Darren's horses had broken from the corral off in the distance. Somehow, the little prairie home had escaped serious damage. Only the chickens were missing, along with the little roof that had hung over the well. Ty had just reached the storm cellar when Darren and Liz emerged, carrying a cantankerous rooster.

"The storm blew old Red right into the cellar door," Liz announced. "Sure looks like he'll need some new friends, though, before we'll have any more eggs."

Fondly, Ty recalled the slender, well-shaped legs he had glimpsed before Liz had disappeared into the cellar seconds before the tornado had struck. "That was as close as a body orta find hisself," Ty said. "Else they would be blowed off the face of the earth." He self-consciously ran his sleeve across his face and his forehead.

Darren dropped the pecking rooster and ambled toward the house. "Looks like we were lucky this time," he said, happily noticing they still had a roof over their heads. "This twister will give Liz something to write about, that's for damn sure."

Liz

At sundown, the endless sky had cleared of menacing clouds, and the orange-and-red globe that was the sun slid from view. Throughout the afternoon, Ty had wrestled with his mixture of mud, sand, pebbles, and straw to set tightly the remaining stones that Darren had wanted around his well; then he set about constructing a new little roof over it. As the day went on, the scattered horses had all drifted back and lazily hung around the corral. Ty had also found the time to repair and secure the corral.

Presently, Darren looked on approvingly. "Well, Mr. McCord, you sure enough fulfilled your part of the bargain—in spades."

Ty smiled tiredly. "I better clean up. I don't reckon a man that's this bad a sight is deserving of one of Liz's meals."

Drawing two large buckets of water from Darren's well, Ty carried them to the barn, setting them beside Grey's stall. He lit a small lantern and proceeded to remove his shirt. He had begun to slowly wash his face when the barn door creaked open. In the dim light, Liz appeared as lovely as ever.

"Don't let me interrupt, Ty," she said. "I brought you something from father: some of Doc Crenshaw's favorite

Kentucky whiskey. Hope you enjoy it. It's only for special occasions. I'm hoping you're prone to a drink now and then. Father guessed you were."

"Well, I'm much obliged." Ty gratefully accepted the cup. "I'm not rightly proper clean yet," he said, enjoying a sip of the whiskey.

"Take your time, then. Get yourself all gussied up for supper." Ty's broad, powerful shoulders and a back that tapered to a narrow waist did not go unnoticed by Liz. Neither did the old shotgun wounds on his left shoulder blade.

Ty fed Grey and brushed him down then put on a fresh shirt. It was his favorite—a double-breasted one the color of red wine. Darren's whiskey was going down smoothly, and Ty took his time in finishing it off. He hoped it wouldn't be his last of the evening. Eventually he made his way toward the house, careful not to forget Liz's cup.

A fine dinner was filled with conversation ranging from the Goodnight-Loving cattle trail to Kentucky whiskey. Ty kept fighting his urge to stare at Liz as she flitted about. Finally she seated herself next to Darren, looking Ty squarely in the eyes.

"I'm quite curious how you came about those back wounds," she queried matter-of-factly.

"You noticed," Ty said quietly. "It happened in Laredo a long time back. There was an attempted bank holdup. I was sent there to get ... *involved*, you might say."

"So you were a lawman?"

"Yes, ma'am, I was."

Darren piped in. "I told you, Liz, he had that look."

"So ... what type of lawman *were* you?" she asked.

"Why, I was a Texas Ranger for quite a while after the war. Spent most of my time in Texas and Oklahoma."

The forthright beauty smiled admiringly. Ty sensed it was time to find out about her before she got more curious; he was uncomfortable enough as it was.

"I figured you are new to this country," Ty stated. "Staying for awhile?"

"Well, Ty McCord, I taught school in the east after I finished my education. I found a great deal of pleasure in writing, so I came to Kansas City. *Scribner's Monthly* was nice enough to buy some of my written observations. After a few months, father wrote me to come further west. I had always wanted to see the frontier. I probably inherited that urge from the two of them."

"Her mother was a brave soul," Darren added. "The second year after we settled in, she fell ill with what Doc Crenshaw described as a growth in her vitals. She was gone shortly thereafter. I've been alone since then, Ty, 'til Liz came from the city. She has been a downright blessing. Tougher than a pine knot if you ask me." Proudly, Darren raised his cup and lovingly hugged her shoulders.

"It sure enough has been a pleasure enjoying your hospitality," Ty said thankfully. "Grey will be hauling me on to Dodge before sunup. He's rarin' to go."

Liz held him with her emerald green eyes. "Listen here, Ty McCord. The Simmonses don't plan on letting you go until you fill us in on the rest of your plans. Where are you going to light anyway? Dodge?"

Ty looked away, all stirred up inside.

"One night in Dodge will do it for us. I plan to drop off some mail, grab some smokes and supplies, then head due east for the tallgrass country. My trail will end there. My sights are set on a ranch with plenty of longhorns. It'll take a heap of doing, no doubt. Say—once I find my grass, I'll send word. Maybe you could write to me now and then, letting me know how things is going out here, Liz. One of your articles would be nice, too. Sure would."

"That's what we'll do then. So take our word, we will write," Darren promised.

"Likewise," Ty said, as he slid his chair away from the little wooden table. "I'd be obliged to help with them pots and pans. Seems the least a man can do after a supper like this.

"Not in this home, mister!" Liz snapped. "You've done enough helping out."

"Well, then I suppose I'll try to get some sleep now." Ty extended his huge hand. Darren shook it vigorously.

"Be careful," he said, putting his free hand on Ty's shoulder.

Then Liz put her slender hand in Ty's, leaning forward on her toes and kissing his cheek. Ty stroked his drooping mustache as she withdrew. "Plan on me writing real soon," Ty said seriously. His words were a far cry from what he wanted to say, but he didn't trust himself.

Sunup was a ways off when Ty crawled out of the hay where he had settled himself. It was raining through the open roof, which was what had eventually awoken him. He was not disappointed, glad to be on the move. He quickly grabbed his easy-riding, western stock saddle with the high cantle that he preferred. The saddle was as much a part of him as was his Winchester. Then he strapped on his peace-maker. Dodge was no place to be without a sidearm. He pulled the cinch tight on the saddle and flipped the reins over the duckbill pommel. Pulling on his slicker, he led the brute out of the barn, noticing a light shining through a window near the back door of the house. It opened, and Liz appeared, holding an umbrella. She motioned to him, and he moved swiftly toward her.

"You'll catch your death out here, woman," he said as the rain streamed off his hat.

"I've got your coffee ready. You better come inside and enjoy it."

Ty snubbed Grey to a small post and stepped into the house. "Father is sleeping, Ty. He's not healthy. It's his heart. I really came out here to coax him into leaving, but he's having no part of it. He's terribly lonely, and that's not helping things, either." Handing Ty a cup, she sat down, running both hands through her hair. "I can't remain here forever, but then again, it's not right to leave him here alone with the brutal winter storms that are sure to come. Furthermore, I have absolutely no business whatsoever asking you, and it will be difficult indeed to honor my request. I will understand if you decline. Especially since we have only known each other for a day and a half. And most of that time was spent either in the tornado or repairing things." She hesitated long enough to sip her coffee. "His leg gives him problems, too, especially in the cold. However, in just this short time, I sensed he might pay attention to you. So here it is, straight as I can say it; will you come back in the early spring to help talk father off this land? He needs to sell out before it kills him."

"Might kill him to leave, too," Ty answered softly. "Being that he put his claim here in the first place."

"That's a chance I have to take, Ty. Will you help me?"

"Shouldn't be a problem. I'll be back here, Lord willing, by early April. See you then." Ty rose from the table and quickly disappeared in the light rain and fog of the morning.

Dodge

Several hours in the persistent rain passed before Ty and the brute trotted along Dodge's main street past a livery stable, a drug store, and a sizeable dry goods and general store. In the four years following Ty's last visit, the town had become much larger. Wagons and horses were everywhere up and down the street. At the north end was a three-story hotel. The Prairie Grand included Ellen's Eat Inn with a picture of a cowpuncher on the door.

Finding a first-floor room, Ty signed the bill and paid for his stay. He then quickly departed and mounted Grey again. He had noticed a new livery stable down the muddy street, several hundred yards from the little hotel. After a quick inspection, he decided it suited the stallion well. The proprietor, a large black man, was pleased, too.

"That's some horse you got there, mister," he said, admiring Grey. "I don't rightly know if this old buffalo soldier has set eyes on a giant like this one. Name's Roy Johnson. What's your name, sir?"

"Ty McCord."

"Long as this beauty is in Roy's stable, he will get the finest treatment on the plains. Count on it, Mr. McCord."

"That's what I hope for, Roy. Sometime before sunrise, I'll be here to saddle him."

"Whatever's your pleasure sits right with old Roy."

Satisfied, Ty took his bedroll and Winchester and returned to the Prairie Grand. The room was sparse but clean, with a single curtain covering his large window. In less than an hour, Ty had bathed, shaved, and spruced up with fresh clothes. Characteristically, his rifle was placed under his mattress, next to the wall. Someone sitting on his bed most likely would not notice it. He had removed Ben's hidden banknotes and secured them in a thin leather pouch under his shirt.

Ty stepped out of the hotel and retrieved a cheroot from his shirt pocket, lighting it and enjoying his first drag. As was his habit, he perused his surroundings carefully before ambling toward a saloon two doors down from the hotel. He could only hope he would find the equivalent of Darren's Kentucky whiskey there.

Once through the oversized batwing doors, he surveyed the room and chose a two-chair table near the long wooden bar, away from street-side windows or doors. He still had enemies from his years as a ranger. In a town like Dodge City, it was a good idea to be careful, especially when a fella was responsible for more than a few men being sent to prison—or to their ultimate reward.

"Whiskey? Glass or bottle?" a barmaid blurted through uneven, oversized teeth.

"A bottle will do," Ty responded, avoiding her stare.

When she returned with his whiskey, she sat on the table so he would have to extend his hand near her considerable breasts to retrieve his glass. "I can be a heap of fun for a man hankering for excitement. Name's Betty Sue."

Ty rolled his cheroot between his fingers, flicking off a long ash. "I bet you'd be a mite too much of a hellion for a feller like me, Betty Sue. That whiskey is what I been hankering for. 'Preciate the drink. I sure do." The chubby girl bounced away to the next table in search of a willing prospect.

Moments later, a large, long-bearded man appearing to be in his early 30s came through the slatted doors toward the overcrowded, long bar where two bartenders were dealing with late-afternoon, thirsty customers. Ty noticed the man did not appear to be carrying a six-shooter under his long coat—unusual for a man in this country, particularly a young man. Finding no slot at the bar, he noticed Ty sitting alone. He quickly moved in Ty's direction. Ty pointed a long finger at him and then at the vacant chair at his table.

"Thank you, sir," the man said gratefully. "I hope you don't mind my joining."

Ty offered a hand. "Not a bit." He noticed his guest spoke with the accent of German immigrants he'd come across in the last few years.

"I am Albert. Albert Bierstadt," he announced haltingly.

"Ty McCord here. Pleased to make your acquaintance. Which way you headed? West, or somewhere other than that?"

"I'm returning from Oregon. Traveling back to the east," Albert answered formally in his broken speech.

"I here tell a man orta make that ride some day. Right pretty country, they tell me."

"Correctly you have been informed, sir. I found it wonderful viewing. The mountains reminded one of Switzerland. Quite spectacular. Along with the beautiful rivers and forests. I will make every effort to return soon, if I'm fortunate enough to find a market for my paintings in the east."

"Redskins a nuisance on that trail?" Ty asked.

"There were only a couple incidents of note," Albert revealed seriously. "Mostly I found them fascinating subjects—colorful and interesting subjects, indeed."

The buxom waitress wandered toward the two men with her permanent smile.

"A beer please," Albert said.

"How you doing, cowboy?" she asked with a wink toward Ty.

"I'm doing fine, Betty Sue," Ty said. She then turned her attention elsewhere.

"The Choctaw and Cherokees caused plenty of trouble for the Texas cattleman. At times, they ended up paying the hostiles fifty cents a head in '57. The next few years, the price got up to seventy-five cents. Stole more than their share of good horseflesh, too. The likes of the Cherokee Brigade is still in business in Oklahoma. As a young man, I made the trip pushing longhorns north through that territory."

The artist listened with interest. "Quite fascinating indeed."

Presently, Albert's beer arrived. "Mr. McCord, would you do me the honor of joining me for a bite to eat?"

"You bet. A man should not eat his supper alone if he can avoid it. I'd like to hear more about them pictures you been painting."

The little eatery was almost full when the two men walked in. Ty eyed the faces around the small room, finding a corner table covered with a faded red-and-white tablecloth. In a moment, a slight Spanish-looking man in an apron approached them.

"Buenas dias, amigos. I have not seen you before. You are surely new to us. You see I am blessed with a good memory."

"I reckon you'd be right as rain. Name's Ty. This here feller's name is Albert."

"Amigos, I am Juan Jaramillo, proprietor. My half-sister Ellen was the previous owner. A good cook, but nothing like my lovely wife, Maria. The best Dodge has to offer. You will soon see."

When Juan returned to the kitchen, Ty noticed that the proprietor's gun belt was visible underneath his apron.

A careful man, Ty mused. Juan soon returned with large helpings of beefsteak, rice, beans, and tortillas, along with a jar of jalapenos, that he carefully placed between the two men. "Much obliged," Ty said gratefully. Ty had a notion he might have seen Juan in the past. *Where was it?* he wondered while devouring Maria's fine meal.

Albert consumed his meal in a formal manner, saying little until the food was gone. "You will be setting out for this tallgrass you speak of soon?"

"Reckon so. I've a notion to make tracks for Cheyenne Bottoms. Not too far from Great Bend. Maybe even Little River."

"The stage returns in two days. I've arranged to take it to Kansas City, where I plan to ship my paintings on to New York, or perhaps Boston," Albert revealed. "I'm in serious need of money, so I can return to the mountains of your west. My desire is to continue my work there for as long as I possibly can. However, the necessity of funds must be first fulfilled. Perhaps our paths will cross again. I've certainly enjoyed your company."

"Likewise here," Ty agreed. "Ain't never met a true artist. Sure enough, been a real pleasure. Hope you find good luck with your brushwork."

Presently, Bierstadt departed for his boarding house, leaving Ty with his thoughts of Juan Jaramillo. Ty paid Juan generously then stepped outside to the boardwalk. The sun had dropped behind the taller of the structures on the west side of the street, causing odd-shaped shadows to creep across the dirt-and-gravel road. Sauntering down the boardwalk, Ty considered a stop at a smaller, congested saloon then rejected the idea. Instead, he located a worn, undersized bench outside a barber shop. On the window, a sign advertised a fine haircut and expert shave for fifty cents. The question of Juan Jaramillo continued to pester his mind. He became more convinced he had seen the man's face and long, black hair in his past. But where or when? He sat observing the various sorts of men and women moving up and down the street and in and out of the dozen or more stores, eateries, and offices. It was a pleasant evening for the citizens of Dodge.

Close by, the familiar sound of can-can music filled the evening. Alone with his thoughts, Ty did not notice an approaching visitor.

"Amigo, it is me," Juan announced happily. He now wore a flat-crowned black hat and a multicolored shirt with pants sporting white stitching down the outside of the legs. On his right side hung a tied-down, silver-encrusted holster with a bone-handled Colt .44 in it.

"Hardly could recognize you without that there apron you had on," Ty stated.

"Si, senor. There are times I'm two men, no?"

"You are someone I believe I seen somewhere else, Juan."

"Perhaps, senor. Once I rode with Sheriff Brice down in Clovis. I was not too old, but he liked the way Juan could handle his pistol."

"Maybe my mind is figuring it all wrong," Ty admitted, stroking his drooping mustache with his thumb and forefinger.

"I work for many ranches in Texas," Juan continued. "Then I joined up with my cousin Pedro. He was a lawman in Amarillo, a deputy sheriff." Sadness was in his high voice. "Pedro was shot dead by very bad men."

"Now it's clear to me! Ranger Lee Hall brought me with him to Amarillo to investigate that bank robbery and killing. Summer of '67."

"That man Ranger Hall, he talked much with me," Juan acknowledged. "I stayed on, wearing Pedro's badge for two years, thinking only of revenge. I thought of nothing except killing those desperadoes for two years of my life. Maria and I grew apart. When my half-sister got sick, I bought this little place. We became happy again. But now

I grow weary of life here, and Maria is often afraid. We talk of our own ranchero; that is our hope and prayer."

"By golly, we crossed trails after all, Juan. There for awhile, I was thinking my remembering faces had vamoosed altogether. If it will do you any good, I can tell you Pedro's killers got strung up. Every one of them. They dangled in Waco."

Juan crossed himself, saying something under his breath. A considerable silence followed before he spoke again. "Soon, the Jaramillos will have laid claim to some land. I dream of some fine land for grazing."

Ty snuffed his smoke under his heel. Suddenly, they heard gunfire in the direction of Roy Johnson's stable. Instinctively, both men ran toward the noise. Rounding the corner at the rear of the stables, they were greeted by the distinct sound of a heavy-gauge shotgun. Smoke was starting to billow out of a window. Inside, wild sounds of panicked horses and the booming voice of Roy Johnson assured them he was still in charge. Men were now coming from all directions, shouting and waving for help, fearing what could happen to the tinderbox town if the fire got out of control. Crouching, Ty cautiously entered the stable, his pistol at the ready. Instantly, he saw Roy down near Grey's stall. Blood was coming from a shoulder wound.

"Thieving sons of bitches should've known better than stealing from me—no how!" Roy shouted fiercely. The empty ten-gauge scattergun was still in his massive hand. All around, buckets of water and wet horse blankets seemed to have materialized. Horses were being quickly led into the street while cursing men lifted watering troughs, turning them over on the smoking straw.

Ty motioned for Juan to stay with Roy, then he led Grey into the street. More help continued to race by, and eventually, the smoke dissipated into the broken sky of the evening. Inside, Juan, along with a large, black cowhand, had gotten Roy to his feet.

"Them drunk skunks stole the money I took out of banker Joe's vault today. I have to pay for my new buckboard tomorrow. It took me a year and half to put enough dollars aside so's I could buy it."

"You're losing too much blood, senor. We must find the doctor soon. Do not be stubborn," Juan urged. "My friend will help us." The round-faced cowboy put his arm under Roy's blood-soaked shoulder.

"I done been shot before in '63, soldiering with the buffalo boys. Didn't like it none then, either."

Ty watched as they shuffled off. Roy had been smart in keeping all his hay supply in one location for just a situation like this one, where quick reaction might just prevent the whole kit 'n' caboodle from going up in flames. Several locals held watch over the horses while Ty looked more closely at the scene. Down on one knee, he examined the dirt around the wide entrance, knowing dozens of footprints and hoofmarks would reveal nothing of interest. Two older punchers had been a few strides across the street from the stables when the shots rang out.

"They weren't riding no decent horseflesh when they a come a bustin' out of Roy's place. We seen one of them slump over when that scattergun went off. One of them boys is carrying a load of buckshot from both barrels. We seen it all. The sheriff and his deputy is gone today. Ain't due back until late tonight."

Ty nodded his thanks while he examined the stable's doors. One of the doors held a considerable amount of buckshot. Blood was spattered on it at about saddle high. Shortly, three more black cowboys arrived, returning the horses to the stables. Bringing in bedrolls, the punchers settled in for the evening. The tallest of them came toward Ty with his hat in his hand.

"I'm Roy's brother; Rondell's the name. Just checked with Doc Settles and ol' Roy is going to be fine—but ain't no way he's going to be fit for work. So I reckon us boys will be filling in. We'd always done it when brother was not around."

Ty introduced himself. "Glad to meet you."

Rondell stood admiring Grey. "That horse is a fine-looking animal. Them eyes is showing a streak of ornery, if I do say so."

"It does take awhile to get to know him."

The hotel clock showed almost midnight when Ty returned. When the commotion subsided, Ty found Juan again and said his good-byes. Juan divulged that he would write Ty if he intended to come east toward the tallgrass.

In the early morning, Ty found the sheriff in his office.

"Those boys won't be traveling far," Ty said. "Roy's shotgun seen to that. Quite a mess of blood on the door tells me they need to find a doctor soon. They ain't riding much, either. My guess is those deputies of yours will have some new guests behind bars before sundown tomorrow."

"I won't be surprised myself," the young lawman said matter-of-factly. "Nobody around these parts will stand for the shooting of Roy Johnson. Just 'cause the man's blacker than the Ace of Spades don't mean he ain't good people. I'm going to see he gets his new buckboard, too."

The sheriff eagerly shook Ty's hand as he departed. "It's been a pleasure meeting a famous ranger like you. Even if you don't tote a badge these days."

Ty touched a finger to the brim of his hat as he closed the door to the jail behind him.

The Table Flat Trail

Ty swung into the saddle at first light, feeling conflicted about the ruckus that had left Roy Johnson shot up and his stable smelling like the aftermath of a prairie-grass fire. Ranger blood was still in him, boiling, and it urged him to find the fools who had stolen Roy's money. Yet that was young Sheriff Tom Wilson's job, not his. Perhaps ex-deputy Juan might step into it if things called him to do so. It was certain he wasn't going to be serving beefsteak much longer with the itching he had to find a spread of his own. Men like Juan weren't reined in for long. Holding up the law on the frontier and trailing steers in rank country seemed more to Juan's liking.

Snorting and prancing in the cool, clear morning, Grey seemed anxious for the trail. Ty held him at bay long enough to find saddle comfort, then he surrendered the reins so the brute could find his own pace. Grey's half-breed bit began its familiar chirping sound, complimenting the creaking of the saddle and the rhythm of his hooves. They rode on toward the rising Kansas sun.

"Grey, the trail to Kinsley, Fort Larned, and Pawnee Rock is going to be flat as Maria's tortillas," he muttered, stroking the flying mane.

High noon found them at Fort Larned. Every mile

along the trail had the sameness of the one before. Next it was Pawnee Rock. The position of the sun in the cloudless sky was the only thing that kept changing, mile after mile. By evening, they had forded the Arkansas River outside of Great Bend, then they made camp five miles out of town at Cheyenne Bottoms. It had been a long, hot ride. Yet the evening was turning out to be even hotter with the stifling humidity. The rare storms that drenched the land of Liz and Darren had not found their way to the Bottoms. It was dry as a bone. The weeds, sparse grass, and stubby bushes cracked when stepped on. This ground had not seen water for a long time, although a tiny stream nearby had an inch or two of water in the lowest spots. Insects buzzed all around until Ty's little campfire took hold, sending smoke into the flatland sky.

"Can't remember when I didn't have to battle the wind out here, Grey," he said aloud while stirring the dry sticks and flimsy bark he'd gathered and dropped into the flames. Lighting a cheroot, he sat down beside his saddle, waiting for his much-needed coffee to boil. Nothing stirred around him as the light of the day disappeared into the orange haze of the western sky. A short time after he had eaten, he picketed Grey near a little patch of dry, flimsy grass. When he returned to his fire, he poured himself a cup of hot coffee, then he set about pulling off his tight-fitting boots.

Eventually, his thoughts returned to Liz, and her proud but unhealthy father. She was a strong woman who would not be easily intimidated or bullied, even on the frontier; she surely would never be outfoxed by any man who came across her. No doubt plenty would want to give her a try. She simply was the most splendid woman he had met anywhere in all his days. To not see her again would be a downright shame. Only slightly less foolhardy would be to pass up an invitation to one of her meals.

Finally, the dark, hot, prairie night evolved into a

symphony of howls, barks, chirps, screeches, and scamperings. Soon he fell into a deep slumber—the sleep of a man who was at home under the stars.

The sunrise at Cheyenne Bottoms once again brought stifling, heavy air and a dust-infested south wind. Ty pulled his hat low and tied a big bandana over his mouth and nose. Hurriedly, he scattered the campfire, mounted Grey, and galloped into the haze of the morning. With some luck, Ty planned on locating the little town of Platter, where he hoped to find his old legendary marshal friend, Travis Doyle, a master conversationalist who had upheld the law on the frontier for decades before turning in his badge for the quiet life of a small spread.

Throughout the early hours, a filthy, hot wind battered the tall rider and edgy stallion as they continued on their way. By early afternoon, the sun blazed down on the beaten trail and withered anything in its path. It was a brutal day to find oneself in the saddle, not unlike many trying, long trails in Ty's past. Through it all, Ty stuck to his plan, urging the mile-eater on and on.

Late afternoon brought a dying wind. Pulling up alongside a rocky little stream, Ty let Grey have his fill.

"Figger Platter ain't but a few more miles, boy," Ty muttered. The land along the trail had begun to change in the last several hours: short grass had been more plentiful; burr oaks, birches, and cedars more common. There were cottonwoods in the hollows. Occasionally, smooth hills would appear, always giving way back to the flatland, then cropping up again here and there as they trailed eastward.

The hot still of the evening had begun when they trotted down the only street belonging to the tiny little settlement. Several rough buildings along the dusty street welcomed them: a feed store and stables on one side, with a blacksmith and a miniature saloon on the other. The dry-goods store and post office were flanked by a rugged, undersized building that advertised itself as a saddlery.

Platter's residents surely did their borrowing and paying somewhere else; there was no sign of a bank.

"Well ain't you a sight for these old eyes. Looks like you captured some dust, so you just brought it with you. Either that, or the only coal mine in this here country has done got itself discovered by one Ty McCord hisself," the old lawman said when Ty slid from the saddle, snubbing Grey to a hitching rail.

"It's been a long time, young man," Ty announced, offering his oversized hand.

Travis, at the age of eighty, was spry and strong, with a neatly trimmed beard and dark, Indian-like face.

"The well's out back. Get yourself rid of that there grit. I'll see to this huge creature. When you're ready, I'll warm my famous rabbit stew. Neighbor lady dropped off some mighty tasty fritters, too."

"You're a savvy old coot," Ty chided Travis, while sipping cold water from a jar. "Why, you staked your claim nowhere near a bank."

"I shot or sent off to prison enough of them thieves to see me through my lifetime—and someone else's, too. Don't fancy bein' near no bank. Horse thieves was the worst of the outfits around here. Gents that was in these parts taking another man's horse was hung. Course you've seen it, too, when you was rangering down south."

"Sure did. Still a bumper crop around." There was a brief silence while Ty refilled his jar.

"Ty, you may a' heard me and Wes Hardin had a run-in once in Abilene," the old fighter went on. "The coldest killer I ever set eyes on. That boy was on the dark side of murder. Cold-cocked the drunken snake and deposited his worthless behind in jail back in '66. He was the worst of any I ever seen in these parts. I never held no respect for folks who shielded the thieving killer neither. In the old days, Cheyennes out here wasn't much trouble 'less them blue coats was in the area, then things got a mite nasty right fast. Custer's Seventh was a burr in them braves' hides. When they was all stirred up, mutilating and scalping was a specialty of theirs. Many a trooper bit his own lead rather than be captured."

Ty was exhausted from the ride and found the conversing a bit tiring. "Sorry, Travis, if you'll excuse me until morning, I got to get me some shuteye."

"Say, I got an extra bed if you care to use it," Travis offered.

"Thanks anyway. Your horse barn is more my style. Besides, I've been told my snoring is almost too much for man or beast."

Only a few minutes passed before Ty was in a deep slumber as the hot night enveloped the town. Sleeping the sleep of the weary, Ty suddenly stirred in his bedroll. At first he thought he was dreaming, but his trained ears told him otherwise. Somewhere near the oblong corral next to the horse barn, the whispering voices of several men could be heard. Ty shook his head to clear it so he could get his bearings in the blackness of the barn.

"It's been ten long years, Barney. Now's our chance to settle the score. Them prison years is different. They don't come easy. I ain't gonna forget the man responsible for putting me in that hellhole, much less killing brother Carl. A man has needs to even a score like that."

"Not so fast, Lou," said another intruder. "A man like him don't forget how to care for himself. There's no need to hurry at all. Rem is due here any minute. So's Tate. You want to be sure, don't ya?"

Ty crawled on all fours toward the voices, sending two rats scampering behind him. Finally, he arrived at a spot in the corner of the stall where he carefully came to his feet. He peered through a small opening between weathered, dry slats in the wall. The men were squatting on their haunches, concealed behind a large water trough just inside the corral gate. They had stopped their talking.

Over a small rise behind the men, Ty made out vague silhouettes of two more men making their way carefully to
the opposite side of the corral. One man, tallest of the
two, appeared to be carrying a short shotgun.

"They's here now, Barney," the anxious one said gruffly.
"Time to get on with it."

A vengeance killing! Ty thought, deciding just how he
was going to deal with the situation. Wide awake now,
he went over his options. Time was short. He would need
his Winchester, then he would have to warn Travis, so he
would at least have a fighting chance. The four men around
the corral would have a need to escape in a hurry. Ty speculated another man must be with their horses somewhere
near. Ty soundlessly retrieved his rifle and stuck his Colt
inside his belt. It became obvious what he had to do. He
needed a clear line of sight, so their movements could be
seen, then he would alert the old lawman to the approaching danger. Ty thought to himself, *They've probably been
watching this old log house for awhile.* Travis only rarely had
visitors. Most likely the widow down the road who gave
him the fritters was one of the few.

The tall one with the shotgun was figuring on a close-in
blast. Finding a window that gave him what he needed, Ty
discovered all the intruders could be seen. It was time to
make his move. He was sweating profusely in the hot stillness of the barn. His wits were about him now.

The tall latecomer suddenly dashed toward the house
then held fast near the rear door. Next, the anxious one
stepped into clear view as he walked calmly toward the
house. Ty was tracking the plan clearly. It was time to act.
The Winchester went to his right shoulder, sending two
quick shots into the rear window. Travis would be awake
now, having a moment to arm himself. The odds would be
getting better.

"What in tarnation!" the man in the open yelled. "Who
fired those shots?" There was no answer, only the raspy

sounds of locusts and fluttering birds. He spun around with his pistol in his hand.

"Get down, you fool! The shooter's in the barn!"

Hurried footsteps went toward the rear of the barn. Ty took note when they halted. He hoped Travis was putting two and two together inside. "Odds still improving," Ty muttered to himself when the man in the open moved behind the well, kicking a spare bucket over.

"Damned idiot," someone shouted.

The handle on the door that led to the crowded tack room creaked open slowly, revealing the knuckles of the turner. Ty moved beside the door, knowing a man always uses his dominant hand to turn a handle on anything. Gun in hand, Ty didn't wait for the door to open further. He brung down hard the butt of his Colt, viciously crushing the intruder's fingers. The man went to his knees cursing and screaming. Ty then stepped into the doorway and smashed the thief's face with a knee.

The night went silent again until a familiar voice from inside the house boomed, "I'm here for the taking, but don't hurt my friend. The man wouldn't hurt a fly." Ty could only smile, slipping into the shadows of the barn directly behind the intruders.

"No deal, Doyle! You both are done!" the anxious one yelled.

All three were visible now while Ty took cover behind a good-sized tree. The door to the house seemed to open on cue; old Travis filled it with a Colt in both hands.

"Don't think about it!" Ty commanded, when the man with the shotgun took aim. "I'll split your skull like a melon. I can't miss from this distance."

Unbelieving, the tall killer raised up to fire. A perfect shot from Ty's Winchester quickly shattered the man's arm. The next one destroyed his knee. Travis casually took the shotgun from the tall one and savagely hit him across the face with it. "There will be no parole this time, Rem," he said loudly.

In the distance someone dashed away through the trees and underbrush, making no attempt to cover his exit. "Let him go, Ty!" the old lawman yelled. "Three out of four ain't too bad when you can hogtie a no-account outfit like the Watsons. I'll find escorts tomorrow. Rem, this time you and your two no-account brothers are going to find themselves in prison for good. Your raping days are finished. No telling, you might find yourself on the receiving end of the raping where you boys are headed. Wouldn't that be a damn shame now."

"Travis, ain't no way for a man to sleep around here," Ty said as they led the men away toward Platter's little jail. "This town don't get your attention right away, but it's a mite too excitin' to suit me."

Beezer

The following day, Ty and freshly shod Grey trotted into the morning, leaving Platter behind. Only a whisper of wind accompanied them. Heavy, hot air hung under a lingering haze. The old lawman had seen to some jerky and biscuits, along with sugar for Grey.

As the mind-numbing day wore on, the new terrain evolved. They traversed grassy hills and then mesa-like plateaus that soon gave way again to treeless vistas. Grey clattered loudly in and out of dry, rocky creek beds along the way. Then they moved into open, flat spaces with stands of big and little blue-stem, buffalo grass and tall switchgrass. Scattered, sparse stretches held on grudgingly as well.

Mile after exhausting mile, Ty watched the prairie proceed to alter itself from a barren panorama of sameness into expanses of soft, rolling grass covering large masses of ground; odd-shaped mounds; and vast, endless, mirage-like stretches of the plains—a massive new land for the lonely rider.

Unwilling to press on in the unforgiving heat of the evening, they stopped in the little town of Rockdale. Following a much-needed cleanup, Ty sat alone enjoying his supper when, unexpectedly, the familiar face of Harper Craig appeared.

"My God, if ain't the famous Ty McCord done lost his trail. Word come to these parts you was heading in this direction, but you wasn't wearing no ranger badge no more."

"Good to see you, Harper. Last time I seen you, you was a bar slave in Fort Worth, taking fine care of them thirsty rangers and pokes. Seat yourself."

Harper was a good-natured man of thick build.

"Looking for tallgrass?" Harper inquired.

"You bet."

"Well, ain't that something," Harper said. "I come here last year when Uncle Jacob Caulton sent me a letter asking for some help. He started raising them Black Galloway cattle near here, over at Clover Mound Ranch. Jacob come here in '60. Straight from Virginy. Same year old Abe was elected president." Sipping his coffee, Harper went on excitedly. "I suppose a man as well knowed as you can wander about anywhere and still be knowed."

"Seems to be the case," Ty answered dryly.

"You figgerin' on settling down in this here grass country in the foreseeable future?"

"Planning it that way, Harper. When I find what I'm looking for, I'll put some stakes down."

After Harper had departed, Ty relaxed in his room, enjoying a cheroot and letting his mind wander to thoughts of Liz. His plan was progressing smoothly since the fracas in Platter, and he looked forward to the short ride through Bronco City to Tanglewood. Hopefully his trail would end there if his plan played out.

The next day Grey pranced nervously while Ty saddled him. Ty paid the stable hand generously then stepped into his worn saddle. The night's welcome sleep had refreshed him, and he urged Grey into the cloudless morning. No doubt a blistering day lay ahead as the heaving, rolling grass became more and more plentiful. The scene was reminiscent of Ty's days spent near the Gulf of Mexico and the rhythms of big water. By mid-afternoon, he had arrived in Tanglewood and established a bank account by depositing his money and Ben's banknotes. Next he had checked into the Grande Central Hotel followed by an appearance in the office of the local marshal, Austin Seward, previously of Clayton, New Mexico. The marshal was a lawman known to harbor a deep hate for horse thieves—a man like many who considered that occupation more serious than murder. His personal preferred deterrent for horse thieves was a quick hanging.

Days came and went, with frequent trips to the surrounding towns of Empire and Green Ridge. It seemed ranchers in the area were pleased to count Ty among their midst, even though he was an unofficial ranger. By the third week since arriving in Tanglewood, he had received mail from Austin headquarters, Ben, Liz, and the Reverend Reyfus Williams. Even a barely readable note from Roy Johnson in Dodge awaited him. Ty set about to dutifully answer each missive. Liz's long letter was full of concern for Darren and the prospects of another brutal winter. She spoke of the loneliness such a winter would bring to both of them.

By late summer, the missing rains finally arrived, drenching parched land. There had been no defense for the drought that had beset the land, only waiting for the winds to transform themselves from hot to cool, bringing storm-filled clouds with prairie-saving water.

Following days of welcome rain, Ty and Grey worked their way through a gaily running stream and into a long, wooded vale filled with birch, cedar, cottonwood, and thick hedge. Scattered hedge balls littered their path. As they went along, they passed round, treeless hills with rock-filled sloping slides that led to thick, grassy tops laced with narrow animal trails. Occasional stands of crimson-leaved bushes served as observation posts for endless varieties of birds.

It was in the little settlement of Beezer a few short miles to the south where Ty was informed of the widow Olson. She had a desire to return to Kentucky to tend to an ailing sister. As he was approaching her little house, he could see a tall, slim woman with her hands on her hips in the doorway of the rock-and-timber structure. Ty approached and snubbed Grey. The woman had a pleasant, fleshy red face. Long, graying braids hung down in front of her shoulders. She wore a long bright dress that almost covered her tall black shoes.

"So you are Ty McCord, are you?"

"Reckon so."

"Well, I've got some cold tea ready. You might as well join me."

"Don't mind if I do. Hope I ain't butting in on your evening or nothing else like that," Ty said seriously.

Inside the little house, they seated themselves at a small, well-made table festooned with a flowerpot full with freshly picked flowers.

"To tell you the truth, McCord, not much goes on here anymore. Mostly I tend to my garden and busy myself playing solitaire. Since Frank died, it's not the same. Matter of fact, I don't do much at all. We fell in love with this land and had plans that were grand. Frank was the kind of man who could make it all happen," she said sadly. "Now I find I'm needed back home, so I'm planning to leave for Lexington as soon as my land is sold."

"Your husband must've been a fine man. I'm real sorry you have to leave these parts."

"In a way it's your gain if you have the money to pay for it. I would feel fine if I knew it was in strong hands."

Ty found himself feeling extremely sorry for her. There was a sadness to her and yet a strong resolve, as well. She was a survivor, where some in this land were not.

"This grass will be saddle high in the spring. There's simply no place on this earth as far as I know more fitting to raise livestock. From what I hear about your previous employment, you're familiar with long, hard hours and taking care of yourself. A man with those characteristics and the gun you have on your hip should do fine here. If you're buying, I'm selling. Almost twelve hundred acres can be yours."

Ty was taken back by her forthrightness. "Well, Mrs. Olson, we ain't talked a price yet."

"I don't necessarily feel the need, Mr. McCord. Men like you don't often make a habit of cheating women, particularly in these parts. That banker in Tanglewood is a good man. He knows this land like the back of his hand. Have you had the occasion to meet up with him?"

"Sure did. Not long ago."

"Well, I've sort of thought you would," she said, satisfied.

Ty went on. "He mentioned he'd see to it that a reasonable loan could be had with what I deposited when I come here last month. I'm figgerin' on raising cattle next spring—if and when I was able to find some land and have it all tied up by then. Before the war, I was a drover down at the Big Matador Ranch. Pretty far out in west Texas. I was thirteen when I made my first drive north. We pushed five thousand head of half-wild longhorns up through the old Texas Road into Sedalia, Missouri. I got a good trail education fast in them days."

"The folks in Beezer said you were quite a gentlemen, Mr. McCord. Yet you told me a lot more than I rightly expected. I appreciate that in a person. This land is yours. I'm leaving it for you to do as you see fit. No doubt my husband will be pleased about now. In fact, I'm *sure* he is."

There was a long silence while both thought about what had just been transacted. Outside in the trees, owls hooted away as the shadows of the evening proceeded to lay themselves on the land. The sad widow eventually spoke.

"I would like to be alone now if you don't mind, Mr. McCord. You finalize this deal with the bank tomorrow. He will handle my end and see that I get paid what I have coming." Ty had begun to quickly make his way toward the little door when she tugged on his sleeve. "A word of advice: you will need a good, strong woman before long. That's just a plain fact. Otherwise, a man might become twisted as the Tanglewood River itself.

"I'll keep that in mind," Ty said as he mounted.

According to the Plan

By the early days of October, marshal Seward had almost given up his campaign to enlist Ty as a deputy, though he held out some unspoken hope for the future.

"Why if the word got out that you was wearing a badge again, most of my problems would be over," the marshal said seriously over a generous beefsteak. "Not to mention I'm damn tired of forkin' up my hard-earned salary trying to buy you off."

"Ain't my problem," Ty said, sipping his drink.

"Besides," the marshal went on, "this here hotel food ain't exactly cheap."

"I sure appreciate it, though," Ty answered with a smile.

"This is big country with big grass. Folks is coming in all these counties by the hundreds. They done had a necktie party up in Waubunsee County—and in Lyon County, too."

"Don't blame them," Ty said grimly. "A man ought not be stealing another man's horse."

"I always did have a problem getting to them necktie affairs at the right time," the marshal admitted, with a sarcastic glance.

"Tell you what I'll do, partner," Ty said leaning back in

his chair. "If this population around here keeps exploding, and this here lawlessness gets a damn sight worse, I reckon you could count on me for piecemeal work."

The marshal was taken back by the sudden offer. "I knew all along you had a heart. I'm much obliged, and I'll sure accept your offer, Ty. Yes, I will."

Presently the two lawmen shook hands, then Ty slowly mounted the hotel stairs to his second-floor room. Before going to bed, he took the time to jot down a brief note to Ben, detailing the transactions he had made with the bank. He sealed the note up for mailing the next day.

Ty rose early the next morning, returned to the small restaurant, and sat down to a stack of pancakes and black coffee. Minutes later, the hotel door swung open, presenting a smiling Miss Olson.

"The stagecoach is due any time now to take me to Empire then on to Lawrence. From there, I'm going to Kansas City, where I plan to catch my train back to Kentucky. Just thought you should know, so you could move out of this hotel."

Ty felt half guilty. "That's mighty kind of you, Mrs. Olson. Won't you join me for a cup of coffee?"

"I'll have some tea I suppose," she said appreciatively. "Mr. McCord, I have left my husband's tools, along with his favorite shotgun. They're of absolutely no use to me. You will find them in a closet just inside the rear door. They're very well cared for."

"I'd like to pay you," Ty said honestly.

"I won't have it, young man. My husband would have done the same."

"I'll treat them with care," Ty said gratefully.

Presently, a stagecoach rounded the corner beside the hotel, trailing dust—along with most of the town's dogs. Miss Olson stood to leave. "I'll just carry your bags," Ty said as he picked them up, heading for the door.

There was considerable commotion around the stagecoach. The marshal had appeared and was helping a wounded man from atop the rig. He was not young and sported a long, gray beard. A blood-soaked towel was wrapped around his shoulder. He swore loudly when the marshal and another helper set him down on the board-walk. "This here run ain't like it used to be," he bellowed. "We got some no-good rascals in this territory. One of them fools up and shot me before Charlie put him down once and for all." He pointed to a burly man carrying a shotgun. "Three of them come out of nowheres, just outside of Casserly. Weren't no older than seventeen or eighteen. Dumber than a rock, too. Wanted the strong-box. When I dropped my pistol down, the dumbass kid bent down to pick it up, and old Charlie there ventilated the boy's chest. Another 'un shot me as they was hightail-ing it out of there. They was sure new in the business."

"Well, Doc Diederich is in today. Why don't you come with me? We'll get you fixed up right away," Marshal Seward ordered. "His office is at the end of the street. He delivered a new baby not more than an hour ago."

Soon, the clamor that accompanied the stagecoach began to die down, and the old driver's wound proved to be a minor problem. Later, the coach rolled off with three riders as escorts for its run to Empire. Ty watched from outside the marshal's office as it rambled eastward.

"Like I was saying, Ty," the marshal repeated. "I will eventually need you around here. Right now, I'll be going to see if I can find that kid with the ventilated chest. It's downright comforting to know you will pitch in. I'll see you soon." The marshal mounted a squared-off, big-headed black gelding then trotted off toward Casserly.

High noon found Ty at his new home. Outside, a per-sistent, brisk wind whistled through the trees and rolling waves of tallgrass. Special care had been taken in maintain-ing his new home. It was neat as could be expected. Even a neat stack of firewood was laid inside the fireplace, ready for a fire—a fine gift from the widow Olson. The horse barn was just as skillfully constructed as the house, by a man who could use his hands. The fence around the corral was strong and in top condition. No detail seemed to have been spared around the entire spread. Ty couldn't wait to check out the fence lines, knowing full well there would be little, if anything, to repair. The following day, he wrote Ben again, describing their new place in the grass.

November arrived several weeks later—and with a vengeance. Early on, brutal winds drove deep, heavy snow through the plains. It was a storm the likes of which Ty had never experienced. Many of the ranchers surely would suffer heavy losses among their herds with untold die-ups, a tragic result of longhorns entangling themselves in fence wire in a vain attempt to flee a blizzard such as this one. As a young man, Ty had witnessed die-ups in Oklahoma. Before his neighbors would be able to rescue some of them, many could likely starve or fall victim to wolves and coyotes.

It was almost another three weeks following the initial assault of the blizzard before Ty rode into Tanglewood, where he discovered there had been five local deaths due to the storm. According to Marshal Seward, one man suffocated in a huge snowdrift after his horse had fallen on him. "That was a good man, too," the marshal related sadly to Ty, as they chatted outside his little office. "He come up from Texas some four years ago with his brother. Bought a spread up near Bronco. They was doing good. Never bothered nobody. Real neighborly type. That horse of his must have busted him up good when it happened. He was saddle-packing a calf he had found in one of them drifts. It's a lousy shame, Ty."

Later, Ty retrieved his mail, picked up food supplies, and stopped for a meal at the hotel, then he paid a visit to the bank before trotting back to his new home. It was bitterly cold. Wind that seemed ever present rode with him. Grey blew clouds of lung-deep steam as he pounded homeward. Once inside from the rage of the wind, Ty hurriedly opened a new letter from Liz. He read it carefully. Any word from her seemed to tug at him in a way that made him uneasy. The letter was full of concern for her father's declining health, along with the difficulties brought on by the early winter storms. The handwriting alone triggered a yearning to look into her bright intelligent eyes. He could almost feel the touch of her soft hands she had put in his only a few months ago.

Two other brief notes had arrived from Ben, and one more from Reverend Williams with news of his growing congregation in Cedarville. Thoughts of Liz hung on as he fed the stone fireplace that soon filled the house with much-needed warmth. Outside, howling winds continued to assault man and beast, piercing even the smallest crevices in the little structure, guaranteeing another long night of bitter, livestock-killing temperatures. Until now, his well-thought-out plan had met his expectations and then some. But no one could have foreseen a winter onslaught such as this one.

The Promised Return

Finally, March arrived beneath a porcelain sky that showed elongated, finger-painted white-gray clouds here and there. The day was windless as horse and rider departed west from their new home in the grass, embarking on Ty's promised return to the Simmons homestead. Dodge was not part of the plan this time; Ty had drawn up a more direct trail over the long winter nights. It incorporated the advice of newfound acquaintances that included a former pony express rider. If the weather held fast, Ty figured that two full days and a morning would work for them. The fewer stops, the better.

Early on, water was abundant along their chosen path, and the sun stayed on their shoulders throughout the first morning. By nightfall, Ty found the safety of a deserted shack close by a stream, where he made camp settling in under a clear night sky. The second day was a copy of the first, with Ty and Grey well ahead of schedule, moving on uninterrupted toward the Simmonses. The rolling hills of the tallgrass country had given way to flat prairie vistas with few disruptions in the western skyline.

Grey seemed energized by the perfect, windless days, almost as if he was as anxious as Ty for the confines of the Simmons place. Liz's deep concerns meant she would expect Ty to follow through on his promise to help her coax her unhealthy father off the land. *Where would they find a new place?* Ty wondered. Would she stay or return to the east and continue her writing for *Scribner's?* It seemed one logical option could be Kansas City, or even further to St. Louis. There was no way to get an inkling of her plans until he arrived and was able to listen to her ideas. He had a suggestion or two up his sleeve if he could actually muster up the strength without making a fool of himself. She was more than a trifle set in her ways. Not to mention making him nervous as hell.

Being near Liz was one thing, but helping make her father pull up stakes was a whole different issue. For certain, she needed a man to hold up his end of the bargain. Then, most likely, she would leave the prairie for parts unknown, where she'd be more comfortable. One day with an unexpected visitor didn't give Ty any stake in her life except this one task. As the following day wore on, Ty concluded the whole thing was nothing more than his word being tested by a fetching woman in a desperate fix. By dark, Ty sat near his small fire, reflecting on their perfect day on the trail and the fact that he was a damn fool.

By mid morning the next day, Ty had caught a glimpse of the little house, not more than a mile away. He wore a fresh double-breasted shirt and a newly purchased bandana, something he decided was as foolhardy as the rest of his situation. Nevertheless, the sight of Liz vigorously waving from her porch assured him she had to have anticipated his arrival to some extent. Her radiant smile and wind-driven hair was just as fetching as he had expected.

"My god, you made it!" She seemed genuinely excited for his arrival. "I wanted so to believe you would return, Ty. That nasty blizzard took its toll on father. Me, too, for that matter. The sight of you and that brute of a horse is truly a blessing. Oh, it is! This will improve father's spirits more than you can possibly imagine." She was truly beside herself with relief.

"Have you visited with him recently about your leaving the place?" Ty asked quietly while he laid his saddlebags on a small stool beside her fireplace. She answered with her eyes, rolling them from side to side, accompanied by a deep breath and set lips. Ty wondered if she had really depended on him, a virtual stranger, to face her father with this matter, but then he thought better of it. She had seemed quite capable of handling tough doings the first time they met. Surely she would not have changed.

After scurrying about fixing coffee, she seated herself by the glowing fireplace. "Ty, would you mind throwing a log or two on? I'll see that we have a hot cup in a minute. I am downright chilled to the bone." Ty stirred the fire's embers, waving his hat enough to start a couple of new flames. Then he carefully added some small logs and slowly fanned them once again.

Liz stared at him intently while he continued to encourage the flames, then she gently touched his arm in a way that made him stop. "Ty," she said seriously. "The fire is fine now. We have to talk. I know you are just out of the saddle, but I have been planning this entire winter, so I'm starting now."

Ty pulled a cheroot from his pocket, lighting it in the fire. "I have been waiting to talk to you, too, 'cause letters don't completely fit the bill. They were nice, but face to face suits me best," Ty said honestly.

"Father almost died, Ty," she announced as she poured his coffee. She retrieved a wool shawl from the back of her chair and pulled it around her shoulders. Sitting down, she held her cup in both hands. "It's his heart. He has trouble with his breathing now. We have to leave soon before he is too ill to travel—if it isn't already too late." There was desperation written all over her face. "You wouldn't have returned if you weren't going to help?" Her moist eyes glistened.

"Yes, ma'am. I figure a man ain't much if he won't help a friend in a downright hard fix."

"Oh, god, I'm so relieved. Father liked you so much. It was the way you carried yourself, he had told me. Saying he sensed you could be trusted. When you departed for Dodge, he bet there was strong odds you would be returning. He had that feeling, and here you are! Goodness gracious, you have made me so happy and relieved."

As was usually the case, Ty was basically speechless. He flicked some ashes off his smoke before taking a generous gulp of his dark coffee. "Ty, say something," Liz pleaded through her gathering smile, showing unbridled happiness for his arrival. Confident eyes held Ty's attention in a way that made him unsettled. This kind of honest emotion was not something he dealt with, except in the presence of extreme danger. There was something in his reaction to her that was quite unfamiliar, a hint of personal need for her to feel safe in his presence. He wanted her to be void of the fear and uncertainty that she harbored. Though she was no doubt a strong woman, she opened her fears to him in her letters and had held on to the hope for his spring return. Feminine words of personal vulnerability were filled throughout those letters that he had read repeatedly during the winter.

Her gaze continued to hold him patiently. She waited for a break in his silence.

"It would be a pleasure to do what I can to help."

"Then you didn't mind begging, pathetic letters?" Liz said honestly, reaching for his hand.

"You use words in a right special way, far as I'm concerned. Don't know a lady that ever carved out writing like you do. Ain't no wonder you was held in high regard by them Scribner folks. Using words is a true hard game that escaped me long ago. I suppose I wouldn't have been riled

up if you would have sent more letters my way," Ty said
with a genuine grin.

Her hand reached his with a small squeeze that totally
surprised him. "Father is gravely ill, Ty, yet I am hoping
your being here will lift his spirit. It did wonders before."
Ty dropped his head, staring at his boots, still holding her
outstretched hand. Words once again escaped him like
birds in a forest fire.

"He's asleep now, but I will wake him for supper."

"I look forward to seeing Darren. I truly do," Ty
admitted.

Liz withdrew her hand and rose to her feet, pulling the
shawl tight around her. "Plan to stay in my bed tonight, so
whatever you have, bring it into the house; it's starting to
rain."

"I don't reckon I understand."

"Well, it's all I can do to be hospitable," Liz said play-
fully.

"Begging your pardon, Liz, but I don't suspect a lady
such as you should be elsewhere. I won't have a bit of that
goings on. *I'll* be the one bedding down elsewhere, for
sure."

"Well, then, Ty, you can have my pallet in father's
room. He needs close watching, along with help to the
outhouse every now and again," she said seriously. At that
moment, Ty grasped her fatigue, finally understanding
what had been hidden between the lines of her heartfelt
letters. "Ty, he hasn't been able to walk without help for
the last three months. It is so very sad." Suddenly the tears
of exhaustion and sadness streamed down her face like a
rockslide. Slowly they fell, followed by a torrent of tears.
Unashamed, she stretched out her arms for him. Ty held
her in his arms while her body shook and shivered. Then
she began to cry more loudly. In moments of brief compo-
sure, she begged for forgiveness for her carefully crafted
letters that pleaded for him to return, which would take

him away from his new life in Beezer. She was ashamed of her selfishness for her own life and inadequacies. "Oh, Ty, forgive me, please." Engulfed in his arms, her body finally relaxed and came close to dead weight. She went on repeatedly exhaling between sobs. Release of the strife in her life was deeply embedded in loneliness. "Ty, it was a godawful winter."

A speechless Ty held her until she was completely spent, then carried her to her bed and covered her with a heavy patchwork quilt. For a brief period, Ty stood admiring her limp, exhausted body as she gently fell asleep. Her expression seemed to be one of contentment. Perhaps there was a hint of subsided relief and safety. He was sure it had some significance for him. What that was, though, he was at a loss to define. An educated, fine woman she was—certainly of different stock than he. Was there something personal in her eyes, or was she merely latching onto a lonely man like himself to save her father?

"Liz, is there someone here?" Darren inquired from his bed in a weak, broken tone. The unexpected voice quickened Ty's attention to attend to his primary duty.

"Why, I didn't pay no attention to you up front," Ty confessed as he opened the unlocked door to Darren's bedroom. "I figured you was sawing logs in your sleep. Didn't want to bother you none."

"Well, just 'cause a man is situated on his backside doesn't mean he's sleepin'!" The voice was weak but still commanding. Ty quickly noticed the neat little makeshift pallet on the floor next to the door. "Well, man, I need help. Things is breaking down in my frame. You mind escorting me to the privy? Can't do it on my own anymore. Liz fell a number of times trying to help me outside. God bless my daughter. She never once complained, but I've worn her slick, Ty. By golly, you are a sight for these tired eyes, damned if you aren't. She needs help as much as I do. This winter had in mind to taking us both down, but

Liz would not give in. I swear she wouldn't, 'til a few days ago when I saw her begin to weaken. I don't know exactly what the word is to describe her, but she's my saint. She's done her best. She don't know what quit means."

When Ty lifted Darren from his bed, he was only a shadow of the man he had met barely nine months ago. Carrying him to and from the outhouse, Ty sensed death in the fragile old soldier's breath. Something in his frail body was killing him; of that, Ty was certain. It was what the pleading, worn, wonderful eyes of Liz had been telling him. She had lived out the long isolation of a horrendous winter on the frontier with impending death and loneliness and waning physical strength. She was totally spent.

Later, Ty left Darren's bedside, returning to the warmth of the fire and a stacked supply of logs on the hearth. They were more evidence of Liz's devotion to Darren's survival. Liz's cold coffee pot was soon returned to hang over the fire. When he had a hot cup of steaming coffee in his hands, he then sat down to assess the options before him. Biting the end off of another long cheroot, he lit it as he stared into the fire. Outside the little house, he could hear the telltale signs of strong, biting spring wind. It was beginning to rain hard now, which reminded him how fortunate he had been to capture unnaturally pleasant weather on his ride from Beezer. Perhaps he and Grey were meant to arrive when they did. Next, he would need to decide on a plan of action for this situation. There was more here than he had expected.

At sundown, Ty hurried to the barn to tend to Grey. A powerful wind was blowing sideways, making a popping sound as it assaulted his long slicker. "This might just be a gully washer, Grey," he said, as the brute licked the sugar from his hand.

Chapter 9

A Killing in Guymon

It was nearly ten at night when Ben McCulloch locked the strong, tall doors to his stables and mounted his little painted filly. The storm that had blown through earlier in the day had finally stopped, leaving the street a trail of mud, along with debris that had collected in the puddles. A big, shaggy hound with three legs watched them as they made their way down the street. A sharp wind snapped at the fringe of his leather jacket. His tired eyes watered as he wiped the light sprinkle from his face.

"Girl this ain't fit for man nor beast. It's fixing to blow again," he said quietly, as he spurred the anxious little paint. A half moon and low clouds provided little light for them.

He had a final stop to make before he called it a day. The old ranger ran his sleeve across his face as they hurried on in the dark, letting the little paint go at her pace while Guymon disappeared behind. The half moon was disappearing, but it didn't matter. The Rockin MH ranch stood less than a mile away. It was along Cut Face Creek, which defined the low ground where the big house was perched. Ben's weekly visit there was the highlight of his quiet existence.

On this cold, wet night, he was looking forward to his

usual hot apple pie and coffee to break the chill in him. Once the ranch came into sight through the stinging rain, he was certain this was not going to be a good night by any stretch of the imagination. The flames he saw lighting the night would not be doused quickly by the rain. The big, sprawling house was enveloped in fire, and they were flames that would destroy the old landmark forever.

The filly raced toward the destruction before them as if she knew where she had been bred. Ben urged her on with thoughts of his old confidante, Milly Nell Hogan. She was a central force among the ranchers in the territory. Oddly, she treated him as a son, even in his considerable years. She always welcomed his presence with tales of earlier days, gospel lessons, or the topics of the cattleman and their women. She held strong opinions with a will of steel. This commanded the respect of all who knew her. Even her detractors held her in high regard. Without a doubt, she bred the finest horses in the territory. She was ninety-six years old.

They galloped on, reaching the tree-covered path leading to the big house. Ben jumped off the filly just as two huge beams buckled and crashed through the floor of the circular porch. Flames engulfed the entire structure, leaving no possible entry whatsoever. Some distance behind the structure, Ben could see smoke and flames destroying Milly's two massive horse barns that were now merely jagged, odd-shaped remnants of what they had been.

A voice rang out behind him. It was Beau Burey, Milly's trusted foreman.

"Ain't gonna be nothing left but the crying," he shouted sadly. "The boys done their damnedest, but it was a loser from the start. I figure some of them horses that didn't burn up may wander back here tomorrow. The rest's been stole by whoever done this. What's more, they surely planned it for some time before they struck us. They know'd this was the night the boys and me eat our supper with Miss Milly. We all look forward to doing that, so we was all putting our feet up, having a whiskey or two, just listening to Milly's tales. Just as it was turning dark, Antonio seen flames coming out of the north barn. It must've been going for awhile, because when we got there, it was already a lost cause. Most of Miss Milly's purebreds is gone. Then all hell broke loose in the south barn when shots began to break out. Antonio went down, shot through the leg. People was coming from all directions, seeing them flames and all. It was confusing seeing who was who. Then some fellers come from out of the dark, they torched the house, but we just couldn't be sure if they was neighbors or not. Besides, they was a big bunch on horseback, and we was on foot and all. I'm pretty sure a couple of them riders is hauling some lead from my men, but none of them went down. When the rain started again, a man couldn't see a hand in front of his face with all the smoke around. Shouts was ringing out for help with the raging fires everywhere, but it was just too late. Nothing much is going to remain or survive this raid."

"Where is she, Beau?" Ben asked anxiously, staring at the mud at his feet.

"She didn't survive it, I'm afraid, Ben. When them lanterns come through the windows, she grabbed her old double barrel and went out the back of the house, yelling and screaming like I never heard. She raised that shotgun to her shoulder just as a rider come out of that smoke and run straight over her from behind. Must've broke her neck. She had been shot, too. Lorna, her favorite of the help, is with her behind that wall, where she always wanted to be buried. Lorna loved her like a mother, 'cause Milly loved her like the daughter she never had."

Together the two grim friends slowly made their way to where Lorna sat, uncontrollably sobbing, still holding Oklahoma's most famous woman rancher. Both men stood solemnly by, pondering their own personal loss. Behind them, the fire in the big house began to peter out. Farther away, the two barns were still burning with a fierceness that no man could stop.

"How do you think this will all settle out, Beau?"

"Well, I ain't quite sure, but one thing's for certain: me and the men will put this outfit back together like it was, one way or another. We owe it to Miss Milly. Ben you might as well know that Milly told me she put me in her will in the event she no longer was around. I'll have it checked out to be sure, but I reckon I'm the new owner, unless she changed her mind."

Another hour went by then it began to rain again in torrents. It was a late blessing for the men and women fighting the flames. Ben trotted off at sunrise to try and find an hour or two of sleep. *The stolen horses might turn up sometime*, he thought. But the Rockin MH would never be the same; and nor would *he*.

Milly Nell Hogan was laid to rest three days later, in the presence of most of the local ranchers and inhabitants, who'd traveled from miles around to pay their last respects. Ben's deep sense of loss consumed him. The day following, he sent a long letter to Ty detailing the raid and mentioning the ear markings used to identify Milly's finest horses stolen: a small H behind the left ear. He knew Ty would keep it in mind, because some stolen horses were often driven north to be sold. Also, he knew Ty would be buying only the best horseflesh he could possibly find. Ty would likely be searching for geldings to make up his remuda. The Cherokee brigade would extract their price from the raiders if the horses were taken north to sell.

Chapter 10

The Prairie Claims Darren

The cold, wet, gloomy days didn't help Ty's mood or Liz's demeanor. They seemed to be driving her toward something worse than exhaustion. The old doctor friend of Darren's was to arrive today, the fifteenth day since Ty's arrival. Ty had prepared himself for the bad news that was certain to come. Liz, however strong, was his other concern. She was determined, come hell or high water, to dislodge Darren off the land. Ty had the feeling it would not be possible. Day after day, Darren was deteriorating at an alarming rate. He didn't weigh much more than Grey's saddle and blanket now. His voice was a shallow whisper. Despite the tears that never seemed to stop, Liz clung to her impossible dream.

"Where is the god-blessed doctor, Ty? Where is he? Why doesn't he come?"

Over the years, many tight situations had come Ty's way. Life-and-death moments had been faced, but presently, he felt totally inadequate to ease the pain and sadness of headstrong Liz. "He's a man of his word, Liz. You told me that. No reason to doubt it now. Try to relax. Calm yourself, woman. I want to help you, Liz. What can I do?"

"Oh, you are a certain fool, you poor man. I put you in

this horrible situation, yet now I'm yelling at you, demanding answers—answers you can't possibly provide. Oh, god, forgive me, Ty. I am so grateful you came back to us. I am just a foolish, out-of-place woman pleading for things from you. You should go back to your beloved tallgrass country. You don't deserve this. I would understand if you and your magnificent animal went out that door, never to return."

Ty stood beside her, feeling awkward and helpless. Words escaped him like a thief in the night. Yet her stunning presence continued to stir him while also making him uncomfortable and unsure of himself.

"Oh, Ty, hold me. Please hold me," she pleaded between her uncontrollable sobs. "I am so afraid. So wrong to need you like this. It was so selfish of me to have you put your new life on hold. Are you afraid to hold me?"

Ty put his arms around her, holding her head to his broad chest. Her sobs went on while she clung desperately to him. It was as if the intention was never to let him out of her arms or never stop wetting his chest with an endless flow of tears, until he made the pain go away forever.

Without a moment's thought, Ty kissed her hair, feeling her breasts heave against his abdomen. Some of her thick hair stuck in the corner of his mouth when he kissed her tenderly once again. While he held her, Ty glanced through a small window, noticing a horse and buggy trotting to a stop outside.

"Looks like the Doc is here," Ty announced quietly, motivating Liz to let go and make a vain attempt to straighten her hair and gather herself.

"God help us!" she exclaimed as she ran to the door.

The stooped-over doctor entered, carrying his ancient black bag.

"Young lady you look a mess. You do indeed. Who is this big feller here anyway? A relative of some kind or what?"

Ty stuck out his hand.

"I'm Tyree McCord, Doctor. I've been helping Darren some. Liz, too, I suppose ... when I can."

The doctor was at least as old as Darren, with shaggy, white hair showing beneath his black Stetson. His round face had bushy gray eyebrows perched above deep-set blue eyes with big, dark circles under them. He, too, seemed exhausted.

"Say, can a man find a cup of Liz's famous coffee today? I've been a mite busy the last few days—not to mention I'm chilled to the bone. A little of Darren's whiskey in that coffee would no doubt be a big help. Doctor's orders, Liz." Liz managed a faint smile as she continued to run her fingers through her hair. The doctor turned his attention toward Ty. "The way I see it, young man, that young lady will go to bossin' the ol' doc around. Now, I just can't have that happen. Good advice for you, too, if you don't mind me buttin' in your affairs. She's stronger than a mule. I suppose it's kept her going out here in this country, especially with Darren's condition like it is. She scares the bejeezus out of them young bucks that come sniffing around her. How long you been here, anyway?"

"A mite over two weeks."

Liz hurried back with the coffee, handing it to the doctor with suspicious eyes.

"What have you been saying to Mr. McCord?" she demanded bluntly.

"Advice of sorts," the Doc offered, sipping the whiskey-laced coffee. "I really can't go on about it right now. I have to attend to Darren." In an instant, he was closing the door to the little bedroom, leaving the two of them alone once again.

"I'll not be leaving just yet, Liz. If you want me to stay, I will help where I can." Her eyes began to tear up once more. Unashamed, she then reached her hand across the kitchen table and grasped Ty's hand.

"Have I made you feel sorry for me? Made you feel

guilty? If that is what has happened, I'm truly sorry. That isn't my intention at all. I can take care of myself, you know."

Ty cracked a wry grin when she tried unsuccessfully to withdraw her hand. "I honestly don't feel none of that," he said, looking into her tired eyes. "You're in a tight spot. I want to help. Them letters you wrote was genuine. Nothing was flowered over. I looked forward to your mail. I read them all over more than once."

"You did?" she asked, surprised. The bedroom door suddenly opened, quieting their conversation.

The doctor emerged, still holding his cup. His face was expressionless as he seated himself at the small table. "There is absolutely nothing I can do, young lady. Rest assured, I would if I could. If that old trooper survives the night, I will be shocked. He has almost no heartbeat. I made certain he's not going to feel the pain tonight. He's a tough one, and he's brave. You know we go back a long ways. He had a rough time in the war years. A fine man by all accounts, Liz. I see him in you, so go and comfort him now. See him through this as best you can." Liz scurried off to tend to Darren. She closed the door behind her as the doctor had done.

"Don't mind if I do," the old doctor said, as he poured another strong cup of coffee, adding a generous portion of whiskey to his cup. "Old Darren always liked the good stuff. I could always depend on it if nothing else. I hear that you was a Texas Ranger folks had heard of back some time ago. Is that so?"

"I reckon it is."

"Your rangering days are over now?" the inquisitive doctor asked, after taking an ample mouthful of coffee.

"That's right. I'm building a herd in tallgrass country; however, I did tell the marshal there that if something got all balled up and clear out of hand, I'd be available."

"You sweet on Liz?" the doctor asked with a wink.

"To tell you the truth, I ain't sure what I am. I come here by accident a year ago, and I can't stop thinking about her. No question she's a real fine lady. I know that much. She's a damn sight smarter than anyone I know, I suppose."

"Well, I ain't dead yet, and I figured you paid some attention to her figure, too. Even at my advanced age, them features get a man's attention. You know it's so— you can't lie to me."

"You're right; I'm not going to argue with that statement," Ty admitted.

"So you like her mind and body. What else is there?"

"Well if she was a horse, she would jerk the reins right out of a man's hands," Ty admitted truthfully.

"Oh, for sure she's got strong opinions. No arguing about that. That causes a feller to shy away. Yessiree. I'll tell you this: a man can't find another out here in these parts that can compare to this lovely young thing. So take my advice—hell, I'm a doctor, you're *supposed* to listen to me. I know these things. Besides, that dying man in there wished with all his heart that you would return to see her. Anyway, you're sweet on her, alright. Probably scared out of your boots at the same time. I figure you're a man who's used to living alone. Just go on and tell her how you see her. She ain't going to be afraid, like you are, to spill out her thoughts and let you know where she stands. I could go on, but enough of this here talk. I damned near forgot to tell the two of you: my nephew is due to arrive in Kansas soon. He's inherited some money from his uncle and is looking to buy some space. You think Liz would entertain a good offer for this place? This young man has frontier fever. I understand he knows farming. He's got a bad case of that disease. Tell Liz when you have a chance. I must leave now. There is a leg not far from here that needs to be removed."

With that, he picked up his hat and headed toward his little buggy. Ty shook his hand.

"Sure, thank you for the advice, Doc," Ty said with a genuine smile.

"Well, I'm chock full of advice, son. People take note sometimes. Then again, sometimes they don't. I'll try to come back day after tomorrow. Nice making your acquaintance."

Ty remained outside in the chill and mist of the day, long enough to see the rig disappear in the fog. Nothing else was in sight.

Back to the Tallgrass

Darren had died quietly the day after the old doctor's visit and was buried next to his beloved wife behind their homestead. Another two weeks of cold, wet, and bleak weather went by before Liz signed over the little spread to the anxious young man from Tennessee.

Ty eagerly helped Liz with the final details, and eventually they departed. Almost three weeks had gone by since Darren's passing, yet Liz still continued to grieve, mostly in silence. Ty had come to the conclusion his role was best served merely by being nearby—except in those moments when she shamelessly asked him to hold her in his willing arms. Long hours of silence often passed in those days, reminding him constantly of his own inability to carry on a conversation from time to time.

Ty felt a closeness to Liz he had never experienced. When there *was* conversation, there was a spirit of deep understanding, a bonding of sorts. Respect for each other's vastly diverse history. A world of wanderlust, violence, conflict, and sorrow filled Ty's past. Now the two of them were thrown together; for what reason, Ty wasn't sure. In the empty space of the frontier, mutual dependence was often the only way to survive. It was what it was—unlikely and random. A reality they both accepted openly.

Prior to their leaving, Ty gathered himself hesitatingly to explain his hope for the two of them in the vastness of the prairie. Liz had long sensed his struggle, and she spoke before he could begin.

"Oh, Ty, I know what you are thinking. I have to believe some sort of divine force from somewhere caused us to be here like this. Was it your leaving Texas? Was it your ranger work or my coming to help father? Was it the trail you chose to Dodge? Was it the horror of the war that drove Darren to this godforsaken place? I know I wanted to somehow experience this new land. Did the killing in your world make it happen? We can never know. Why should we waste our time any longer trying to understand? You are going home, that much I know. I'm glad we are together, Ty. Oh, and another thing: I think I am in love with you. There, I said it!"

Ty placed his massive hands on her shoulders, then she reached for him. Once more her beautiful eyes began to flow. "I tried time and time to tell you, Liz, but I was just plain tongue-tied. I swear I was. You come from such a different place. In my mind, I was certain I wasn't good enough for you. I reasoned you needed something more than me. Someone with book learning I could not possibly measure up to. For certain, I have wanted you day after day, Liz. I need you with me. Fighting the feeling hasn't worked for me. I love you with all I got and more."

As the sun was rising, they still clung together. The agony of Liz's winter had begun to slip away, replaced by the hope they would remain together forever. As for Ty, there was a contentment about him of which he was not familiar.

"Liz, I just can't wait for you to get a glimpse of the place. It ain't very big, but it's sturdy. Out in the grass, there's plenty of springs, so we will always have water for the livestock. *Our* livestock! A good creek winds through our land, too, with lots of cottonwoods, birches and cedars.

My dream is to add to the herd when we get back. This nasty weather is bound to help the grass this spring. Sometimes it grows shoulder high. Saddle high ain't unusual, neither."

Liz sat with a heavy quilt wrapped around her, watching Ty as he dressed himself, finally pulling on his familiar tall boots. He stirred the near-dead fire and tossed in several logs. Standing before the hearth, warming his back, he vigorously rubbed his hands and lit his cheroot.

"The rain is clearing up. Might just prove to be a fine day for going east, Liz. I figure that's a real good omen."

Outside, the orange glow of the rising sun appeared. It highlighted the gray low-to-the-ground haze that was hovering just above the stubble of the dormant earth and the rough rails of Darren's corral. Lung fog blew from the nostrils of Grey and his two companions; one was a black and white pinto, and the other was a smallish chestnut gelding keeping his distance from Ty's brute. Soon, Ty felt Liz's closeness as she wrapped her arms around his waist and rested her head on his back.

"Father has to be so pleased. I have to believe he is watching us. No, I know he is. Do you believe father is looking down on us? With his big smile and all, no longer showing the agony he suffered all those months. The pain is now gone forever, Ty. I never felt so helpless through the ordeal. I was powerless, inadequate, and truly afraid until you stumbled into our lives. Father took heart when he saw the way I looked at you. You didn't seem to notice, but he was so very perceptive. When I wrote you, he read my words, sensing something different in the way I always labored over the lines. That was something I never did when I was writing for the newspapers or to the family. However unlikely and brazen, I simply wanted you to return to us—for *both* of us."

For several moments, there was no sound whatsoever except Liz's muffled sobs. She tightened her arms around his waist, holding on desperately. "Was the eleven thousand the young man paid me enough?" she asked seriously.

"That price was fair for lock, stock, and barrel," Ty answered. "Your two big trunks will find their way to the tallgrass when the stagecoach comes through Windville about two days yonder. Doc Crenshaw was right: that young man was a good feller. It was a square deal."

"No bickering on the price at all?" Liz asked.

"No, ma'am, not a bit. Paid with a guaranteed banknote to boot. That's a fair shake if I ever seen one. He was in a real hurry to get things settled. Doc Crenshaw said he would see to it that things was handled properly."

"Ty, I signed off on it so quickly. It was the last chapter of father's and mother's lives. It's all been so difficult. I'm certain I was up to the whole matter out here, but now I feel I failed them in so many ways. I could've done more for father. I'm just sure of it."

"That ain't exactly the way Darren explained it to me, Liz. He said you did more than anyone could have possibly expected. He repeated it many times. Your kind of devotion was a godsend. He called it 'unusual grit.' He loved you for it. I do, too, Liz. They tell me this last winter's blizzard was the worst one in memory, and it sure was not a time for any woman to be alone with the burden you carried."

"Thank you, Ty. I pray I am never alone again. I won't be afraid, because you will be there with me."

"You bet I will. We're going to be together in the tall-grass."

"I packed mother's trunk as well as mine and tidied up the house for the young man. Some of father's whiskey goes back to Doc Crenshaw. We have several bottles, too. Those times when father shared with Doc were special for both of them. I love Doc Crenshaw."

"The day is looking like we're in for some right nice traveling weather. Grey sure is rarin' to go. That's a fact."

High above, in clearing skies, strings of geese were honking their way north. By afternoon, Liz and Ty, with Grey and Liz's little rust-colored gelding and pinto, had progressed through Windville, stopping only long enough to sign over the title forms.

Nightfall found them checked into a small hotel in the town of Medicine Lodge, where news had reached of a brazen, military-style nighttime raid that had occurred at a large cattle ranch on the outskirts of Pratt. Two ranch hands had been shot down, and a large number of horses had been stolen. The place had been torched, according to the hotelkeeper.

After a welcome meal, Liz, exhausted from the day's ride, went quickly to bed after assuring Ty she would be fine while he was in Foley's Palace next door. Ty drank his whiskey and enjoyed a smoke while he took in the conversation around him—a habit that had served him very well in his ranger years. Rumor had it a similar raid had taken place in the Cherokee Nation just a few weeks prior, resulting in the death of a prominent woman rancher. Evidently, one of the raiders had run her down.

Following an early breakfast, the two travelers rode toward the rising sun into a new morning surrounded by a cloudless blue sky.

"Every inch of me is sore," Liz revealed, as they rode along. "There just isn't anything on me that doesn't hurt."

"I recall you was determined not to ride the stage or that buggy you sold in Windville," Ty replied, smiling.

"I regret that decision, Ty. Dear God, I do so regret it."

"Well, Doc made it plumb clear that from time to time you insist on holding the reins. He advised it's best to let you have them. He said it would make life easier for a feller like me."

Liz adjusted herself awkwardly in the saddle then fixed

her eyes squarely on the trail ahead. She said no more while her little rust colored gelding trotted on.

By nightfall, the two riders reached Tanglewood, where Ty arranged for Liz to stay at the hotel. After spending the night at his new place, Ty and Grey returned early the next morning into town, where he found Marshal Seward packing his pipe and examining some official papers on his desk.

"Welcome back, stranger," the marshal said as he lit the pipe. "Hear you brought a lady friend. Coffee?"

"I don't mind if I do, Austin. You know if the Justice of the Peace is handy? I'm going to need him tomorrow or the next day. Liz and me are intent on getting married just as soon as possible."

"Why not today if we could find him?" the marshal asked from behind a generous cloud of pipe smoke.

"Well, there's two reasons: Liz is simply too sore from the ride. She ain't never done a ride anywhere near that long, but she wouldn't have it any other way. You could say she's got a right stubborn streak running through her. Right now, she's more than likely soaking in a tub. The other reason has to do with a wedding dress of her mother's. It's due in here on the stage tomorrow, along with her other belongings."

"I see. Sounds like your lady ain't no wilting flower."

"You could say that."

Working the Spread

"Dear, it's everything you said it would be. I am so happy. I have never been so content."

It had been almost two full months since the marriage had taken place, with Marshal Seward as the best man, along with several nearby ranchers as witnesses.

"With you here, Liz, this is all a man could ask for," Ty said softly, as they watched the evening sun slip behind rolling green hills in the distance.

Once inside the house, Liz busied herself with hanging family pictures, while Ty's thoughts returned to Ben's most recent letter revealing the details of the raid that indeed had taken place near Guymon in Cherokee Nation country. It had to be the same raiders he had heard about in Medicine Lodge. Most horse thieves he had dealt with were far more discreet in their style, working in pairs or by themselves and as far away from folks as possible—odd goings on in the prairie, especially in the Nation. Rustlers with that many horses would have to find buyers nearby and have the horses hidden carefully—a big challenge for the raiders in the wide-open spaces of the prairie.

The weeks of late April and May were surprisingly ideal, with adequate rain and warm, sunny days. The bluestem tallgrass was getting an impressive start. It was an unusually fine spring for building a herd. Ty's herd was getting bigger almost by the day, as well as the ever-busy Liz's flowerbeds. Neighbors often came by to visit with Liz, some with young children who had taken a liking to Liz's lemonade, which was always available. A large, black dog had taken up residence on their back porch, along with several stray cats that preferred the horse barn, which was just far enough away to avoid the dog.

Returning from a long day in the grass, Ty found Liz carrying water from the well. Her long hair was blowing wildly in the constant wind. She waved and smiled. Quickly, he relieved her of her pail, and she kissed him on the cheek. Ty wondered if any man could possibly be more content or proud than he was at that moment.

"The marshal stopped by this morning, Ty."

"What did he have on his mind?" Ty asked, tossing his gray hat in an empty chair.

"He didn't say. He did tell me one of the hands on the Bellemere spread got run over by one of their bulls. The boy has several broken ribs, along with a broken leg."

"Sounds like he will be hurtin' for awhile," Ty remarked. "It happens. Good thing it weren't his neck or back. Being a hand is rough business."

"Darling, you have dealt with other things worse than that. Will you ever talk to me about those times? I need to know all about you. Sometimes you talk in your sleep. It scares me to no end when you yell out. More than once, your sweat came clear through the blankets, yet you never woke up at all."

"Forgetting ain't always worked. I got some leftovers from the war. Say, this venison stew is the best I ever tasted. I could do with another helping, if you please."

Liz fetched the stew and more warm bread. "It's not the stew I want to talk about, but I won't bother you anymore. Just know I want to understand. After all, a wife deserves to be a wife in every way. Father could talk about the war. He always said it was of some relief to get it out in the open. You don't seem to be able to do that."

"Not today."

"Well, when I married you, I wedded your pain, too," Liz said demandingly.

"What I'm carrying ain't fit for a lady to hear."

"I will damn well decide that for myself!" Liz shot back angrily.

Ty pulled away from the table. "I got plenty of work to do."

"You sure do!" she shouted as he hurriedly went out the door.

Something banged against the door loudly. It sounded like a pan of some kind. Whatever it was, it made him smile as he mounted up and headed in the direction of his newly arrived steers. While he moved along in the bright sunlight, a part of him wanted to return to hold his new wife in his arms. Another thought was to keep his distance until sundown, which might be enough time for her to simmer down. He eventually stayed with the latter choice, finding plenty of work.

The afternoon seemed to fly by before he once again headed for home. Stepping into the tiny kitchen, he immediately took notice of an open bottle of Darren's whiskey sitting on the hearth next to a newly constructed small fire. It was a welcome sight indeed. Liz seemed to have disappeared for the moment. Ty lit a long, black smoke prior to pouring himself a short glass of Darren's best. Everything around him was neat and tidy. There were flowers all around arranged in small vases and jars.

Presently Liz's hands were on his shoulders. They smelled uncommonly good. Ty reached across his chest for one of them.

"Mrs. Mehrer and her boy stopped by this afternoon. They invited me to go to town with them. My, that young man is a large fellow. A druggist was traveling through town, too, and I bought some hand cream. Like it?"

"I sure do. Darren's spirits fits the bill, too. You still mad?"

"Somewhat. You don't talk enough to suit me," Liz answered coyly.

"How's that?" Ty inquired, rolling his smoke in his fingers as if he was inspecting it somehow.

"I don't know enough about your deepest thoughts. Your hidden parts, the ones you keep under lock and key."

"It's best they are kept there where they belong."

Liz seated herself on the limestone hearth, holding his hand. "The blackberry wine is in the storm cellar. Do you mind fetching it, Ty?"

"We having visitors?"

"Well, I'd like some for myself."

"You would?" Ty was taken aback.

"Yes!"

"Well, I ain't ever see you partake; didn't guess it at all. I didn't know." Shortly, he returned with a sizeable jug that appeared somewhat small in his hand.

"It was buried, so it's cool. As good as can be."

"I hope so, Ty. There's not much under this dress. I hope it warms me up properly."

Smiling broadly, Ty fingered his smoke again, keeping his eyes on Liz. She sipped the dark wine, pulling her shawl about her shoulders.

"Tonight, we are going to get your past out from lock and key, where I can see it. Then I will know you as I should. All of you is what I'm looking for. That is what I need to be a whole wife for you and myself. Then, of course, we will have all that out of the way when the baby comes." Liz drank a little more wine, waiting for his reaction.

"You want to have a child sometime soon?" Ty asked,

helping himself to more whiskey then passing the glass under his nose.

"I think so. Being a mother appeals to me. I'm ready as I'll ever be, at age thirty-one. You will be a good father someday, too. This place will be fine for a child to grow up in, don't you agree?"

"Truthfully, I ain't ever thought too much about it. But having a son *does* have a certain ring to it."

"Ty, for God's sakes, you don't get your choice. You get only what the Good Lord gives you. Have you noticed that I've had strange cravings lately? I've been wanting pickled beets, gooseberry pie, and now this wine. Unusual, isn't it?"

"Now that you mention it, I *have* noticed. Sure don't hurt your figure none. You have never looked more fetching. What I am thinking now don't have much to do with your eating habits or a lot of talking."

"Damn you, Ty—listen to me! We're going to have a child this fall. Most days when you're gone, I'm sick as a dog. It's been going on for a month. Isn't it wonderful? It's so grand that I'm going to be a mother. I saw Dr. Diederich today. He said there's absolutely no doubt about it."

Ty was completely taken by surprise. "How could I have not noticed, Liz?"

"Oh, it's okay. I don't notice things you do around this place sometime, either. Just promise me you will open up to me. I want each of us to have no stones unturned whatsoever. For me, it means everything, Ty."

"I'll need a generous amount of Darren's best, but I will try my darnedest."

"Oh, dear. I don't want anything in our life unsaid. I don't want any secrets between us ever." Teary eyed Liz reached for him. Ty enveloped her shaking body with his long arms, holding her tight.

"Most men like me don't generally stay hitched or

claim children of their own. They ain't fit for that sort of life. You think I'm worthwhile enough to be a father?"

"I know what kind of man you are, mister. You will be a fine father no matter what happened in the past. Together, we will work to make our child safe and sound in the tallgrass. Oh, I'm certain we will."

By sunrise the next day, Liz felt as if she must be the happiest woman on the face of this earth. She now had a complete understanding of her husband: His war years as a sharpshooter and the killing it brought about had left deep marks. Ty had been a gifted marksman. Many men had died as a result. The deaths remained deep within him and burdened him greatly. Their night's discussion had also revealed him to be without remorse concerning his ranger days. Ben's rangers had been his family—something he had never previously experienced in his life.

Ty stirred when she rose from their bed.

"Oh, Ty, I am so blessed we found each other. My prayers have been answered. I waited so long, but yet here we are in this beautiful country. As God is my witness, you are my big sunshine. What a father you'll be, Ty—I know it. In the past, you did what you had to do, just as my dear father was ordered to do. We have this new life and a child on the way. What more could we ask for?"

Departing the Nation

"I'm of a mind to mount up now. I ain't dealing anymore with those stinking, thieving Cherokees. Besides, a man has to figger they's more than a few lawman on our trail. Going back to the Nation after we got ahold of them Kansas ponies was our only option. Now I conjured up a new intention, so we can get away from dealing with those no-good 'skins. We give 'em too many horses to say nothing about the money they done took just to stay in these parts. I tell you, we're going to move out of the Nation once and for all. I ain't taking it no more." The savage look on Sim Collins's scarred face left no doubt with the men scattered around him that the departure was imminent.

"Come on, Sim, we ain't had no rest since we stole them mounts in Kansas. The men are all done in."

The talker was tall and lanky with a narrow, sunken face; a shaggy goatee made it worse. Peak Gillen kicked the dust at his feet. He was full up with Sim Collins not listening to his ideas of finding some women and whiskey. Two black-handled Colts hung low on his hips. A spent cigarette seemed permanent in the corner of his lips.

"Keep your damn mouth shut, Peak, or I will shut it for you. You don't do nothing anymore but complain."

Sim started to walk past the several men sitting close

to the sullen Peak. His face had become more flushed than ever. The "HD" brand on his forehead seemed to almost light up in the blazing afternoon sun; being branded as a "habitual drunkard" had happened to more than a few young Irish volunteers. The captain that had ordered Sim to be branded had died shortly thereafter from a single shot to the back of his head; Sim had seen to it during the '61 rout at Bull Run.

Sim carried his thick frame on quick, agile feet, advancing closer to the surly young gunslinger.

"I see it this way, Peak. You're no coward, but you are damn sure a fool. Most folks in our line of work end up swinging in the breeze or shot dead. If you've got a hankering to make a play for me, now is the time to do it. Maybe you'll get lucky. This outfit might just be yours in that case. Elsewise, you can leave here and now. Go find yourself a squaw and a bottle. You come back to this here outfit, I'll kill you. What will it be, boy? I've got no more time to listen to you running that mouth of yours!"

Hate raged in Peak's small, wide-set eyes as he considered his fate. Sim was calm. Almost relaxed. A faint grin slowly took place across Sim's craggy face as he stood three strides away from Peak. The other men began to move away from the line of fire, saying nothing. Sim put his thumbs in his belt, waiting. Not a whisper of wind was available. The minute that passed before Peak's lips moved seemed like hours to the anxious rustlers. Gunshots sometimes invited visitors, and they did not need any attention to their whereabouts—particularly to the Cherokee braves they knew were somewhere close by yet unseen.

"I'm staying, Sim!" Peak shouted angrily, while he swallowed the rest of his words. The old, dirty denim shirt Peak was wearing was drenched in sweat.

Sim said nothing more. He turned his back on Peak as he walked away. Death had been close at hand, and he was relieved. Peak was his best man with a gun. Later, after sundown, Sim began to lay out his new plan for departing to the Kansas prairie.

"Listen up. I'm talking to you now. From what I can tell, the majority of them Kansas Injuns is easy to deal with. A bunch of them tribes is farmers, downright peaceful, and ain't horse stealers unless some idiot tries to attack a squaw," he said, looking squarely at Peak. "If a man don't kill their buffalo and leaves 'em be, it ought to be downright ideal up there. At least for a *time*, anyway. Lawmen are scarce as a hen's teeth. We done outlived our welcome among them Cherokees. Not to mention we done left them ranchers real sore."

"Boss, I ain't got no doubt about this new situation like you tell it. How did you find out about them parts? Being you was raised back yonder in the east?" It was Zeb Hernandez, a new rider from New Mexico, who queried Sim.

"You, bein' a newcomer, don't know about my time in Bell Aisle Prison—my whole troop that was captured at Bull Run. The only officer I was ever friends with was in that hellhole with the rest of us unfortunates. He hailed from the south and went to West Point for his schoolin'. He said he often visited Kansas. He had relatives who started some of the early ranches up there in the prairie. He died at Bell Aisle in '63. They wasn't so successful in starving old Sim to death, though. After that, I done some jail time in Memphis with a kid that hailed from a place called Coyville. He went on about Kansas tallgrass territory. Later on, word come that he got hisself hung because he was a horse thief. He was dumb as a bucket a spit." Sim's talking drew to a close while he rolled himself a smoke.

"I hear they got a few lawman in some of them Kansas towns, like Wichita, that would just as soon shoot a body as look at him." It was Breed who spoke. He was normally a rider of very few words. Breed was Breed because he was half Lakota. As far as the men could tell, he had no other name.

"We all heard them tales, but we ain't headed in that direction," Sim shot back. "I've been in them parts years back, but not for long. What I seen was real inviting. Besides, you boys need to listen to the entire plan, not just the half of it, before you start that yapping. Listen here now: We got ourselves a friend up in Abilene. He ain't no ordinary friend, neither—a railroad man with a real need for horses. Not just a passel. I hear he has got a mighty big appetite for as many horses he can get his hands on. My contact is reliable. We done a bank job once in Missouri. He is one of the railroad man's top hands. He's working for the feller that's ramrodding the Kansas Pacific Railroad. Lives like a king at a place somewhere outside of Abilene. The boss don't ask no questions and forks up top dollar for good horseflesh. He hauls his horses in rail cars. Some of them end up as far north as Canada and as far south as Mexico. It don't make no difference to me, no how. It's a plumb slick game, 'cause people ain't surprised Cole Clifford, railroad big shot, seems to always fashion a huge remuda on his spread. His hands are real helpful when it comes to keeping his business private and nosy people at bay. Rumor has it that Luther Taylor and Arch Clements is on his payroll. Seems they rode with Bill Quantril when Lawrence got burned to the ground in '63."

Sim surmised by the men's expressions that there was general agreement. Surprisingly, Breed spoke up again.

"Sim, how we going to find out if this here Clifford is for real? Breed don't like being where he can't trust nobody."

Sim couldn't help but notice that Peak was nodding in silent agreement with Breed. He would have to convince the two of them. Having already considered the possibility, he congratulated himself for his preparation. The remainder of the men would fall in line when Breed and Peak threw their hats in the ring.

"Couldn't agree more, Breed. Don't find the question a bad one. 'Careful' is my middle name. That's how we got to this point. At first light, you, me, and Peak is making tracks for Abilene, and we're going to take some horses with us. Sim ain't no careless businessman. Firsthand knowledge is the only way we make sure we ain't being taking in by a downright thief." Sim smiled broadly, savoring his own cleverness. There was a nasty arrogance about him that made controlling the men a mite easier at times like this.

Unexpectedly, Jake Quinlan chimed in. "If a man can divvy up a bigger piece of pie and get rid of them Cherokees at the same time, I say Sim's game makes plenty of sense."

Jake was small in stature but quick with a gun. Sim's best rider, the little Texan was reliable when things got tight. Sim had never seen a man handle a horsewhip like Jake. It never hurt to have a man like Jake in his outfit.

It was late in the day when Sim sat down to his plate of beans. The sky was dotted with small tumbleweed-like clouds traipsing past the low-hanging sun. Things were much to his liking at the moment. Pieces were fitting together just as he had hoped.

The men would need to be paid when he returned from Abilene. The remaining horses and riders also would need to find a well-hidden hideout within the rolling hills of the wide-open country, where a crafty man such as Sim could become rich and respectable.

Railroad Business

Sim found Cole Clifford a tidy, seemingly careful man. The massive ranch was just far enough from the hustle of Abilene. A long and winding road had led Sim, Peak, and Breed to a wide, one-story stone ranch house. An over-sized porch wound around three sides. Baskets of flowers and vine hung from the porch's roof. Out in front was a buckboard with a handsome, ink-black filly tied to the rail. A deep, tree-infested valley was visible in the distance behind the house. No cattle or horses of any kind were visible to the three riders.

"A man could hide an army in that valley, Sim," Breed remarked admirably.

Once inside the house, Cole Clifford introduced himself and set about explaining his willingness to deal with Sim.

"Boys, I am a busy man, so let's get to the situation right fast." Cole was tall and well attired, with handmade boots that showed his initials on the outside pulls. "My men know horseflesh, and I pay top dollar for good stock. We don't buy jugheads and the like. Delivery is mostly on the same day every time, because of the scheduling of the Kansas Pacific. I have several sources, you see, and deliveries at the appointed times allows a man to run his business effectively and schedule deliveries on the other end. All parties are informed when the proceeds of these transactions change hands. You see, I avoid confusion at all costs when I do business the Kansas Pacific Railroad way—that is to say, *my* way. Any questions before I return to town?"

Sim admired a man with style. "Your men put the horses we brung in your corral. We plan on being paid today! As a businessman myself, I like the idea of a schedule for the future. We want our money today."

"Collins, I don't pay for a delivery without a complete inspection of the goods. Period. I'm real careful that way. So why don't you boys go into town, have yourselves a real good time. Come back in the morning. Now, if you'll excuse me, I'm expected in town to dedicate a new city park I donated. They will be striking up the band before you know it."

From the expressions on Breed's and Peak's faces, they did not like this twist one bit.

"I reckon we'll stay right here where we are. We feel a mite easier when we're close to our horses that ain't been transacted yet," Sim said emphatically, wondering how many of Clifford's men were nearby.

"Now don't get your hackles up, Collins. You come highly recommended as a trusted and worthy businessman," he said, smiling as he straightened his coat on his slim shoulders. Sim's quick anger receded slightly.

"Tell you what Collins, I'll set you boys up with a room or two at my hotel. The whiskey will be on me. Talk to my man behind the bar about a lady if you are of a mind for some entertainment in the privacy of your own room. Name's Daniel. Wears an eye patch, and one arm is missing below the elbow. He serves 'em faster than any man with *two* good arms."

Peak's suspicions had disappeared completely. Breed even seemed to be less tense when he gave a slight nod to Sim. Confidently, Cole Clifford rose and walked toward the impressive front door, picking up a wide-brimmed hat off his brass rack. He carefully positioned it to suit him atop his head of long, flowing, gray hair. Sim thought about the offer, realizing that a man sometimes has to give a little to possibly gain a lot.

"Mr. Clifford, I'll make an exception to my normal way of conducting business. You can expect us tomorrow by no later than ten o'clock." Sim took into consideration two or three hours to round up Peak before they could return.

"Fine then, Collins," the railroader said. "I have a reputation to protect in matters such as these. Hope your evening is to your men's liking. Daniel will take real good care of your needs. Trust me, he is quite accommodating."

———

By the time Sim had his morning coffee in his shaking hands, Breed was at the rail in front of the hotel with the horses he had retrieved from the livery stable across the street. A yellow slice of rising sun was visible through hanging, white-blue, muslin-like fog. Breed was a man who avoided alcohol; it was the Lakota in him.

"You look bad boss," Breed deadpanned, as he threw his saddle blanket on his tan horse.

"Go to hell, Breed. There's a wasp nest in my head. Must've been bad whiskey that one-eyed barkeep poured. Seen Peak?"

"Not since I seen him stagger out of that saloon across the street," he answered, pointing to a dingy, square structure opposite the hotel. "He had a round lady on his arm that looked like she was three times his age. Ugly as Peak—and just as drunk, if you ask me."

"Soon as you get that saddle just right, go find that crazy fool."

A short while later, Breed found Peak on the floor of his room. Locating a water bucket, Breed filled it and pitched it on Peak, flushing away some of the vomit on his shirt.

"Get off the floor, you idiot. Clean yourself up. No way you're going to delay our deal with Clifford. Sim's in a bad way this morning. He ain't going to fool with you."

"He don't scare me none, Breed."

"That's why I called you a fool, Peak. Sim would just as soon kill you as look at you. You bring along anything with you but a thirst?"

Peak rubbed his shaggy head. "Got me a shirt in my saddlebag, I think."

"Good. Sim wants to be there early so we ride out of here in just a few minutes."

"I'm real sick, Breed. It ain't right to go when a body is sick as I am."

"You don't show, then we will for sure find out if you're afraid of Sim, won't we."

The mist still lingered in low spots when the three men rode out of Abilene. A cur of a dog followed them to the edge of town then lost interest as they trotted off toward the Clifford ranch.

When they arrived, a pretty Mexican woman served them black coffee in mugs while they waited on the veranda for the arrival of Cole Clifford, railroad man of the Kansas Pacific. The obscured morning sun gave a hint of rain. Sim was edgy and in an uncertain mood, while Peak and Breed kept silent and suspicious. Soon, a light rain began to patter on the porch roof. Just then, Cole appeared from inside. Beside him was the one-eyed, one-armed bartender, Daniel.

"I trust the evening went well, gentlemen," he said confidently while finding a chair for himself. "It's a safe bet none of you boys is going to be disappointed by this rain. Looks like it could last awhile. Hope it does."

Peak showed a wry expression and nodded at Daniel, still feeling the victim of the whiskey he had eagerly accepted.

"I didn't hear your other name no time," Sim said suspiciously.

"Van Dusen is my last name, Mr. Collins."

The bartender appeared like a quite dangerous man. He wore a much-used shoulder holster and Colt underneath his left arm. Breed stoically confirmed that Sim's suspicion was one he shared.

"Well, businessmen such as yourselves shouldn't be snagged here much longer," Cole said casually. "My boys said we should do more transactions in the near future. Your bunch of horses is as good as I've ever seen. Our customers are particular. Daniel and I agree. So it's top dollar we plan to pay. Those ponies didn't come from around here. No one has seen anything like them. Therefore, we are willing to pay eighty-two dollars a head for those beauties."

Sim was ready to bargain, even though the eighty-two dollars a head was considerably more than he had expected, not to mention it was a price he had never been offered. Peak and Breed remained expressionless but no doubt anxious for him to agree to such a lofty bargain.

"As a rule, I don't normally take to dickering with a man such as yourself, Mr. Clifford; however I have certain business obligations I must meet. My partners put a lot of faith in me representing their interests. I am sure you can understand in my line of work a man can get hurt sometimes, even killed. A lot of risk is involved in this here high-grade merchandise. I just can't bring myself to accept a penny less than ninety-five dollars a head."

Sim had never been prouder of himself now that his prospects had risen considerably. He had made it clear it was not going to be easy pickings when it came to dealing in high-grade horseflesh. A quick glance at his two men told him they were in disbelief that he could turn down such an offer. Sim could only imagine Breed had already conjured up some strange force that had caused him to go plumb loco.

Daniel spoke up bitterly. "I don't think I like you much, Mr. Collins. Eighty-two dollars is more than a fair price. You insult our offer, plain and simple. I can assure you, you will not find a fairer offer anywhere between here and Denver."

Sim slow-rolled a new smoke as he stood up, pushing his soiled gray hat to the back of his head. Newfound confidence fueled him.

"That may be how you view it, Van Deusen. Make no mistake, we got business elsewhere to attend to. Sounds like we can't cut no mustard here. Sometimes, two professional parties can't find no common ground and is better off taking their merchandise elsewhere. Much obliged for your hospitality, but we best be on our way so as not to be behind on our next delivery. Just show us where the horses we brung is, and we'll take it from there." Breed remained stone-faced, while Peak appeared he was becoming sick again. "I ain't dickering no more."

"End this hogwash! I tell you what, Mr. Collins. I have a liking for a man who drives a hard bargain. Especially when he delivers the goods," Cole Clifford interjected, seemingly fed up with the whole scene. "You deliver the other half of the inventory you say you boys are holding, I'll meet your price—if, of course, the quality does not go downhill. Daniel started to protest then thought better of it and disappeared inside. "In fact, I'll settle on half right now." For an instant, Sim felt as if he'd been hit with a broad ax. Then, just as quickly, his confidence steadied him, like a man who had broken his first horse.

"It is a real pleasure to do business with you, Mr. Clifford. We aim to return in four days with the rest of the bunch," Sim said calmly.

Breed continued to be speechless until the three of them stopped to water the horses. The light rain persisted, and the men found shelter under a stand of broad sycamores. Sim was consumed with his prospects for the future.

"The difference between old Sim and losers in this game is real simple: I think big when it comes to dealing horses. No matter who we do business with. Sim don't get taken advantage of by no big shots like Cole Clifford. Ain't nobody going to hornswoggle me; no way, no how. You boys need to pay attention when I'm cutting a deal. Could be you might learn something about how to become a real success in our line of work."

The three riders returned in the late afternoon with news of the deal Sim had cut. By nightfall, the light rain had ended. Hidden beneath a deep-sloping hill, conversation was alive with the deal for more horses. Sim sat alone, listening to the chatter, knowing he'd be taken far more seriously in the months ahead. At this rate, he'd surely become a rich man—a man of means that lesser men would admire and fear.

DT McCord
(Darren Tyree)

By the time November leaves began to turn, the McCord cattle herd had grown to over five hundred head. The previous months had been ideal, with frequent rains that tempered the relentless winds and filled the streams and creeks with life-giving water. Everywhere, the bluestem was high and thick. The prairie ranchers had not had it so good in decades.

On a cold, bright, and windless day at the end of the month, Darren Tyree McCord came into the world kicking and screaming; a big chunk of a boy with sparse, red hair and large feet and hands. Ty held him gently while Doc Diederich finished his work.

Liz smiled, brushing her tears away. "My God, Ty, we have a son! If only daddy was alive to see this child with his bright blue eyes. He hurt like the dickens when he finally came, yet he is the most precious thing I have ever laid my eyes on."

Afterward, Dr. Diederich made his way out the door, saying to Ty, "she needs a couple of days or so of solid rest, Ty; you make *damn sure* she gets it. Liz is a mite head-strong, but that big baby was a tough one. You see to it that she stays in bed. I'll be back in a few days.

Darren Tyree's name had been the result of much debate prior to his difficult arrival, with Liz taking exception to several of Ty's suggestions. Darren Tyree was a compromise struck with the help of considerable debate.

Life soon changed dramatically within the McCord household with the arrival of DT. Liz had begun to scurry about like never before, while Ty became sleep deprived and somewhat of a pain for Liz.

"Don't you have some work to do," she snapped as she rocked their new, loud family member.

"I suppose with winter coming on us. Is he okay? You need me for something?" Ty offered seriously as she shooed him out the door.

It seemed to Ty that almost overnight, he'd been relegated to a second-class citizen, only needed in the earliest hours of the day. Resigned to his new status, he found solace in splitting more logs and stacking them neatly inside his barn. All and all, his first months as a new father proved to be quite puzzling. As the days went on, most of the trees surrounding the ranch became almost barren, with the exception of the oaks, which held onto their brown and yellow leaves. Much of the tallgrass was a rusty golden color. The plum thickets became sparse, and sumac leaves had turned red all around the ranch. Riding fence became only a diversion, since no real repair was needed, and Ty had stacked enough wood for two years of blizzards.

It was during the months of August and September that his remuda had grown significantly, as the result of purchasing a small, adjacent ranch. He hoped by spring his cattle herd would be one of the largest in the county. Soon, further help would be necessary.

On two occasions in November, Ty had noticed a lone rider on a rock-infested hill to the east. If it had been a neighbor, most would have waved or stopped in for conversation. No nearby rancher needed to inspect the place, since all had seen it during his Fourth of July celebrations and the early fall horse sale that had been held on his ranch.

Could be just a curious passerby—or maybe not, Ty thought at the time. Nonetheless, the sightings had stuck with him and his cautious mind. It would be worth mentioning to Marshal Seward if he was around when Ty went into town for supplies. Since the war and his ranger days, there were certain sightings that stuck with Ty; this one did.

Eventually, little DT had begun to sleep through most of the cold nights, and Liz regained her fetching ways. Days and months went flying by. It was a day in early February when Marshal Seward stopped by for a cup of whiskey-laced coffee. He pulled his wild rag down from his nose and seated himself in front of Ty's blazing fireplace.

"Don't mind if I do," he said graciously, when Liz handed him his cup. Holding it in his weather-beaten hands, he looked at Liz and DT. "By God, that boy is some little feller, alright. Growing like a weed. He'll make a fine lawman someday," he said, sipping his brew.

"Over my dead body!" Liz protested.

"What brings you out here, Marshal?" Ty inquired. "It ain't just a cup of coffee. Not on a day like this."

"Right you are, Ty," the marshal responded. "Well, I'll get right to it. I'm in need of a little help. I'm recalling, some time back, you agreed if I ever had a problem, you'd be available. So I come to ask for help, pure and simple, begging your pardon, Liz. There just ain't enough of the law in this part of the territory to go around. Too much space and too few badge toters."

Ty sat patiently while he bit the end off of a long smoke. He glanced at Liz and the baby. "Things was a whole lot different when I gave my word back then," Ty announced, lighting his smoke in the fire.

"Sure 'nough is, Ty," the marshal agreed.

"What is the special need?"

"Horse thieves. Busy horse thieves south of here.

Sheriff Kelton from El Dorado got throwed off his horse and broke four ribs and his shoulder on his gun-hand side. Worse yet, his only deputy up and quit when some drunk shot him in the knee. So between here and Oklahoma, with the exception of Wichita, there ain't much law anywhere. Ark City, Eldorado, Latham, and Eureka all been hit lately. The law in Wichita is already spread too thin. You could say I'm up a creek without a paddle. These raids have all been when the weather is at its worst and at night. Seems they's got a mighty hefty appetite for horseflesh in big numbers. Well over a hundred horses have been reported stolen from some of the larger spreads. All within a day or two's ride of here."

Ty studied his long smoke, checking Liz's face through the haze.

"Sounds like there must be a slew of them, and they're downright bold devils. They gunned down a woman rancher in Cherokee country. A man's got to figure there's a ready buyer somewhere in these parts. They can't just sit around and hold that many horses."

Ty recalled the reported raid outside Medicine Lodge, when he and Liz had passed through on the way to Beezer. "Reckon so," Ty agreed, still searching Liz's eyes. "If a man's word don't hold, then it ain't worth a plugged nickel."

The troubled marshal held his cup in both his hands, darting his eyes from Liz and the baby then to Ty again. "My guess is this here horse county is in their plans. Makes sense, I suppose."

Eventually, Liz broke into the conversation.

"I don't like this one single bit. Us with this beautiful baby and all. You know Ty won't refuse, Marshal. But that doesn't mean I won't hate every day that he's involved. His lawman days are supposed to be over and done with."

"I know that, Liz. Doggone it, if it had been possible, I wouldn't have come here today. Keep in mind, too, this ranch has the finest remuda I've ever set my eyes on. It might be a target some night."

"True enough," Liz agreed reluctantly. Liz's agreement didn't relieve Ty's troubled mind. Conflict with her was something he had definitely wanted to leave behind, safely buried somewhere in the recesses of his nimble mind.

"You got yourself in a tough situation, marshal," Ty said gruffly. "What'd you have in the way of a plan?"

"More men, I reckon. I got a few folks to chat with tomorrow. I'll be returning as soon as I can. That ranger badge of yours is going to help me a damn sight more than you realize."

"You holding back something a feller ought to be aware of? Such as suspicions or something you ain't quite square on?" Ty asked honestly.

"Well, I hear tell there's been single riders sighted coming and going around a few of the big spreads. I ain't seen 'em with my own eyes, of course, but considering the events of late, there's no reason not to believe the other ranchers are being scouted—if that's what you're driving at, Ty. Especially the remote spreads."

The big ranger listened quietly, savoring the last of his smoke. As the marshal's words flowed out, the image of the single rider he had noticed on the round hill returned to his consciousness. It seemed the anxious marshal had a handle on the problem as he went on.

"These boys is smart. I have to believe they know the law is real shorthanded, unlike when they was in Oklahoma with them Cherokees. No doubt the law is on their trail for killing that lady rancher. They might view Kansas as easy pickings."

Liz watched the two lawman, resigning herself to the situation; she could do nothing to prevent Ty from sticking to his commitment to the desperate marshal. She loved Ty for what he was, yet she hated the fear that had begun to raise its ugly head. Little Ty and the quiet existence they had were now at risk. Not given to this sort of intrusion, she felt deeply vulnerable with the prospect of Ty's absence—even if briefly, much less an extended affair.

Sometime after the departure of the marshal, the new parents sat silently watching their sleeping new family member. Ty could sense the fear in Liz; strong as she was, little Ty had changed her as nothing else could have.

"I'll have to help take care of this here mess. Maybe we'll stir up more help, too. These ranchers will have none of this, Liz. There's far too much at stake. Besides, we have plenty of warning." Ty hoped she believed him.

Chapter 16

Bluestem Prospects

Indian summer brought a cold wind to the deserted, half-mud, one-room house that sheltered Sim's men. Jake Quinlan's high-pitched voice held the attention of those sitting around a fire that was sending smoke out the sizeable, jagged hole in the sorry remains of a roof. Jake was a humorless rider not given to tall tales. The little gun-slinger, however, possessed exceptional eyesight that had often amazed the riders, even Breed. "Three days I milled around that tallgrass country, must've set my eyes on more than two dozen spreads. The space between some of them ranches set me and my little buckskin on a riding binge or two, I'm telling you boys. Why, them hills and buttes is such that a body could make hundreds of horses disappear for years. I seen plenty of water, too. Some of it is spring fed, by golly. The boss, he ain't just a whistling Dixie about this grass country. I seen some big farm spreads whilst I was in them low valleys. Why, I'd kill for a place like some I found."

Breed spoke up. "You done enough killing in Oklahoma, Jake. Got the law all riled up, so we had to vamoose."

Jake spun around to face the big Indian. His quick hands dropped to his sides, touching his Colts. "You can rot in hell, you half-breed bastard," Jake said menacingly, his bright eyes flashing in the firelight. "A body lies six feet under in Del Rio because of that pig sticker you been carrying around."

Breed sat down comfortably, cross legged, picking at the fire with a long stick, causing orange sparks to infest the escaping smoke. "The man called me something a feller got to take exception to. Got what he deserved. Lakota blood was spilled by a coward. He had to die. You shot that old lady dead, Jake. You didn't have to run her down, either. That gun of hers was no threat to you from that distance. Lakota don't shoot old women," he finished viciously.

"You ain't all Lakota, neither!" Jake yelled.

Slowly, Breed rose to his full height, towering over Jake. The men remained silent. All the while, Sim watched with an amused half smile, enjoying the scene. Jake canted his flashing eyes upward to meet the unblinking, dark eyes fixed on him from above. In an instant, Breed kicked him violently in the groin, sending Jake off his feet and arching backwards like a half moon. The hardened point of Breed's boot sent excruciating pain throughout Jake's crumpled body. He screamed for an instant before losing consciousness.

Peak then sprang to his feet to examine the unmoving form of his friend. "You might've killed him, Breed. Now it will be a long time before he can ride. So he ain't no good to nobody," Peak said angrily.

"Fools make trouble no man wants. Sometimes get killed. Jake won't die this time. Doubt he'll forget this lesson, neither." Breed's utterings were sad words. Presently, he lifted up his saddle and blanket and disappeared into a nearby thicket. No one cared to follow his silent steps.

"Well, then," Sim Collins said happily. "It's high time to plan the next delivery. Looks as if we have plenty of opportunity staring us in the face. According to Jake, there's some mighty handsome remudas just waiting for us. Most of his sightings was done at sunup or dusk. Plenty of fine horseflesh is available. Outside the little village of Beezer along a creek named Sharps was of particular interest, according to Jake. Says he took a real close look one night. Must have got the best of him. He told me he had never eyed a finer remuda in his young life. He'd tell it this minute to you boys if'n he wasn't groin-booted to sleep."

"At first light, we make a wide sweep, moving north into this grass country, so's that we can settle on a place to hide more horses than we ever had in Cherokee country. We might just hit a mother lode for our next delivery to the famous Mr. Cole Clifford. Them Yankees at Fort Leavenworth is a hard two days' ride to these parts. A man like Sim here needs a certain degree of comfort in order to carry out his work. That amount of distance fills the bill. I figger them blue coats is no threat to us."

The next two days of exploration led to a general agreement for holding hundreds of stolen horses. Some thirty miles from the closest settlement, it looked as though a powerful, unknown pardner had carved stone-strewn, tall mounds with banks that slid into a vigorous stream, thick with cedars, cottonwoods, and sumac flourishing among the thickets that were invaded by strange-shaped little trees growing horizontally from the drop-offs, seeking the sun with odd-shaped limbs. These features formed a natural, mammoth corral hardly visible from fifty yards away. There was only one way in and out. Heavy, unruly undergrowth had formed a natural barrier at the lowest points along the creek. Only the smallest of creatures would find their way through it. Natural piles of deadwood created by spring storms rendered the low spots virtually impassable. Two round, mostly treeless hills hundreds of feet tall protected both the northerly and easterly boundaries with a squared-off butte standing high to the south.

A huge, jagged bluff angled vertically into the creek that meandered through the impenetrable growth.

Sim stared at the surrounding hills. "Any unwanted visitor traipsing over that butte yonder or these sparse hills would be fixing to get hisself shot. 'Cause there ain't no place to hide up there," he announced confidently. "A man don't realize the possibilities a situation like this presents to an enterprising businessman like old Sim. I'm figuring more than two hundred horses could be held here! Plenty of water and grass, too. Ain't much short of perfect for the work we're lookin' to do, *and* it's a lot shorter ride to Abilene from here. All the better for us in this here enterprise, I reckon."

Sim watched excitedly while his men shifted around within the space, examining here and there.

"Boss, we couldn't find no better hide anywhere I ever seen," Peak tossed in loudly. "It's a dream come true, as far as I'm concerned."

Sim smiled a wicked smile of agreement. "You ain't wrong. You and the boys is going to work at sunrise. We'll be needin' to find a right nice passel of horses for delivery to our friend Mr. Clifford and his thieving pardners on that there Kansas Pacific rail line. Ain't no reason this here enterprise won't be a downright success here in this grass. I'm fixing to set my eyes on them remudas Jake seen, but the time ain't just right yet. We need Jake to lead us."

Gathering for Delivery

The prospect for long-term success in the hills and grass was the talk of his men as they prepared to ride into the cold breeze of a foggy morning. In the weeks that had passed since the location of the natural corral, numerous scoutings had been made in an effort to identify the best opportunities among the remudas sighted. Twenty horses had been stolen along the way, but now was time, Sim had explained, to get serious about the horse business. As usual, such work was to be done during the long winter nights by targeting the most vulnerable ranches first. This was followed by what Sim had described as a cooling-off time.

During this period, Peak was to spend time in the town of Tanglewood, where a marshal resided. His deputy was unavailable, making him the lone lawman in the county. That news had been music to Sim's ears. There was no better time to start gathering up his next delivery to the famous Cole Clifford and the Kansas Pacific Railroad.

Big Pine Ranch was selected as the first target. It consisted of a shabby little wood house protected, on the backside, by a steep hill, as well as a shallow stream running a few yards in front of the house with a corral across the stream. The house was poorly constructed, as if it had been put together by a blind man. Sim's men had spotted a huge, flabby man that moved painfully slow to and from his shabby barn that seemed to be on the verge of collapse. A large, white-haired woman had been seen once hanging clothes on a line. There was not a soul in the area except for a ranch some twenty miles away.

"Them horses is real good. Don't make much sense," Dusty Nelson said as they got underway. "The place is a wreck really. Yet he's got them great looking rides. A body would think a much finer place would make more horse sense."

Dusty was an athletic rider from Raton who had left plenty of trouble behind in New Mexico. Sim had favored him from the time he had arrived, because he asked few questions. Handling the horses was second nature to him. Powerfully built, he tackled the toughest jobs with ease—a good hand to have around when there was work of any kind that needed to be handled.

"I come by there twice at night and once in early daylight. Them horses is cared for, and it's strange that nothing else is." Dusty was predictably short with his estimations. "We can take 'em all in a heartbeat, boss. The creek is up, too—a perfect setup. It's a good bet them horses is for sale anyway, so we'll just do it *for* him. That old man sure as hell ain't no rider."

Sim agreed. While the morning developed, Sim's men would scout their way to a rendezvous point atop a tall hill near the Big Pine spread. Dusty led the men, taking care to avoid large, open areas. In the distance, turkey vultures circled a wooded, low field, patiently waiting for their prey to take its final breath.

"Sim, that fat glob don't even have no dog. I swear it is a strange setup. Bothers me a touch." Dusty's cautious nature was always just beneath the surface of his words, a habit Sim had grown to depend on time and again.

Eventually, a reluctant sun popped in and out of smoky

gray clouds as they went on their way. The misty fog that hung over the grass provided them a convenient shroud of invisibleness. High above the riders, unseen geese were honking their way south ahead of the coming winter storms. Mostly they rode in silence, stopping occasionally to water the horses.

By midday, the sun had burned off the shroud of fog, but their well-chosen route allowed the men enough cover to proceed with confidence. Sim and Dusty were the first to dismount once they reached the rendezvous site. They waited another two hours for the remaining riders to arrive and report what they had spotted along their chosen paths. There was a strong opinion among the men that they had arrived unnoticed—a view Dusty Nelson did not share, as was his suspicious habit.

Among the scattered pines, they bided their time, waiting patiently for the covering darkness of the night. Breed sat alone and motionless away from the other men. Soon, a light, cold rain began to fall. In Sim's mind, conditions couldn't possibly be better. Quietly mounting, they rode confidently down the hill toward the Big Pine ranch.

The rain came on forcefully, making it difficult to see much at all. Arriving behind the flimsy barn, it seemed certain they could not be seen from the house on the other side of the stream. Setting about the job, Breed quickly opened the gate to the corral, ushering sixteen horses into the darkness. The other riders rode alongside them to prevent them from scattering. Slipping inside the barn, Breed discovered three more horses. There were two palominos as well as a black stallion. Quickly, Breed led the three out into the rain to join the others.

Slowly mounting his horse, he brought up the rear of the escaping remuda. Close by and hidden by a large outcropping of rocks and thickets, Sim decided this caper was slick as they get. Everything had come together, and yet this was just the start of things to come in the tallgrass country. A man in this line of work couldn't ask for more. Well before sunrise, the men were sleeping soundly within newly constructed shelters inside the confines of their hidden corral. Breed, predictably, was not among them.

The following morning was crisp and sunny, bringing about a close inspection of each horse they had stolen. The men were all in high spirits, with much debate concerning their remuda. As Dusty had promised, the horses were of fine quality; not a one of them had been neglected.

Zeb Hernandez seemed unable to take his eyes off the black stallion. Sim was watching Zeb stroke the powerful neck of the horse. "Don't even think about it none, Zeb," Sim ordered. "You ain't going to ride him anywhere. These here horses is for selling."

Zeb couldn't help but recall that Sim was riding a horse from the Hogan raid in Oklahoma, but he held his tongue. He was not about to cross up Sim. Zeb was a rank, hard veteran of numerous cattle drives. He liked the look of things just as they were. Trouble with Sim made no sense, although he was a man Zeb would never like or trust. He would continue to keep his thoughts to himself.

Several more cold weeks passed, during which the riders completed all four sides of their rough shelters. They seemed to take pride in the work. Mostly, the sunny days served to motivate them to prepare for the coming winter months. Another week went by in which a long and low, well-constructed tree-covered structure was completed. It was built tight against the north confines of the hidden corral, protected by the hill behind. A good number of the stolen horses had taken to it right away.

A quiet period of time followed, during which Jake Quinlan had begun to ride again. He made certain to give Breed plenty of space. Jake would bide his time for now, but the score would surely be settled in due time.

The next ranch Sim had planned to call on was six hours' ride from the Big Pine but only half that distance from the hidden base of their operations, as Sim had begun to call their corral. Daily posted lookouts so far had not seen a single human being. Sim delighted in their comfort and the fact that the oncoming winter would provide what was needed to build the next delivery. A few days later, they rode off to the east, with Jake Quinlan proudly in front. He was eager to point out the prey he had spotted.

Nightfall came with unusually dark clouds and the predictable sign of winter delivered by cold, north wind. Visibility once again was limited—always a welcome ally for the riders—as they drew near the tree-protected ranch house; its lonely silhouette was just a short distance now. They could see a light shining through the windows and smoke curling from a small chimney. Sim sent Peak and Zeb on ahead of them to make certain of a safe approach. Sim prided himself in his calm, confident nature. He was convinced it had kept him alive during and after the war years.

Somewhere near the house, Peak and Zeb remained well hidden in a copse of trees, as the men approached a small, sloping hill where more than a dozen horses milled about in a fenced pasture. One of the riders deftly opened the wide gate and led his horse into the dark expanse that held their prizes. Two more riders swiftly herded the horses out the open gate and into the cold winter night. Peak, followed by Zeb, appeared in the blackness, trailing the escaping figures. Nothing could have been easier on this night of gathering rides for Cole Clifford.

Deputy Ranger

"Come right on in, marshal. You'll catch your death out there," Liz advised, closing the door behind him. The marshal seated himself comfortably by the fire, while Liz hung his hat and sheepskin coat on the kitchen wall.

"Don't mind if I do," the marshal said gratefully.

"Now, you just relax while I tend to Darren McCord." Soon, the loud crying stopped in the bedroom. Liz returned, seating herself next to the marshal. "Ty's fetching some wood. He will be back directly." Liz knew this was no social visit. The marshal looked to be in a grim mood.

"How's that little tyke getting along, Liz?"

"Well, you know he has begun sleeping through the night. Ty's mighty grateful for *that*, I promise you. Ty's been taking awhile to adapt to the baby's ways. Sometimes we are better off if he just doesn't get in my way—if you know what I'm driving at."

"I do, indeed," Marshal Seward acknowledged. "I wasn't much good at that sort of thing myself."

Liz was a little startled by his comment. "I didn't realize you were a father, Austin."

"Me and the wife was real young when I come home from the war. I settled just east of Kansas City. Her name was Ann. We named our baby Charlie. Shortly after he was born, Charlie caught the fever. The doctor just couldn't save him. He weren't even six months old. Ann and me was terrible heartsick. She just couldn't pull herself out of the gloom, so she up and headed to Ohio where she come from, hoping her mother would be able to help. Her stagecoach stopped in Springfield, Illinois, so the folks all stayed in a new hotel that night. There was a bad storm that evenin'; or sometime in the early morning, a bolt of lightning struck and set the place ablaze. She never made it out, Liz. At nineteen years old, I lost *her*, too."

"I had no idea, Marshal. We are truly sorry."

"Truth is, I never told nobody. Most people got their own lives to tend to," he said solemnly.

Momentarily, Ty appeared through the door, popping the snowflakes off his hat. "It sure enough is blowin' and snowin'. It liked to blowed me over out there." He helped himself to some coffee and sat down on the hearth. "What brings you out here on a day like this, Marshal?"

Liz watched the men carefully. She'd recalled the marshal's most recent visit only a short while ago. As far as she was concerned, nothing good was going to happen as a result of his stopping by now. Slightly disturbed, she decided to get up and leave the two men alone.

"I'm a mite shy of help. Seems like my part-time deputy done up and left for Denver. Got hisself a job with the Pinkertons. He was a good, reliable man. Can't blame him, though, for leaving. Pinkertons pay real good, and his wife is in a family way. I been checking around. It appears no help is coming this way soon—at least no *experienced* help. I went so far as checking with the lawmen in Kansas City. There ain't no reason you can't work for me, since you gave me your word."

"I recall well enough," Ty said, flicking snow dampness off his mustache. "I recall, alright. Thing is, Liz is going to be madder than a wet hen. She's more than a handful when her dander is up. Got a temper like I ain't seen before."

The marshal continued. "Ranchers been reporting a fair number of stolen horses. Three come in right before the first of the month. Nobody seen the thieves, as far as I know. Could be that bunch has come up from the Cherokee territory. Then to I hear tell some boys seen more single riders around here keeping their distance in the evenings. It's hard to tell if it's true or not. Who's to say they have a thing to do with stealin' from local remudas. God knows I done all a man can do to find some help, Ty. Fact is, it just ain't available. The law is stretched to the limit."

Ty tossed a hefty log into the fire, "You sure are 'tween a rock and a hard spot, Marshal. I'll do what I can until this situation gets cleared up. Liz is going to pitch a fit, I reckon."

"No way I can thank you enough, Ty. Why don't we hook up at the Big Pine Ranch this afternoon? I hear it was hit first. The setup there practically invited horse thieves. That poor old codger will be a broken man. Them horses was all he and Edna had in this world."

Long after the marshal had made his exit, Liz found Ty composing one of his frequent letters. This one was addressed to Juan Jaramillo.

"Come spring, I reckon we'll be in need of another hand around here, Liz. He'd make a good one for sure, if he's of a mind to come this way. This herd of ours is going to do a heap of growing, and Juan was itching for tallgrass country."

"I know you had to take this job for now," she said. "You best take good care of yourself. DT and I need you more than you may realize. I don't like one little bit of this. When this is all over, I will not stand still for one more minute of lawman work." Ty noticed she had been crying. "If I wasn't crazy in love with you, I'd kill you," she shrieked.

"I'm scared right out of my mind," Ty stated slyly. Then she slapped him hard across the face.

On the Lookout

The weeks after the visit to Big Pine brought two new reports of missing horses and yet no sightings whatsoever of the thieves. No question these men were careful, well-organized riders with a large appetite for horseflesh. As near as Ty could tell, as many as sixty-some horses had disappeared. It wouldn't be a simple task to keep the stolen horses out of sight from prying eyes, either.

"Well, for my money, I'll lay odds they go back to work soon to take advantage of the long nights, along with the fact that no ranchers have seen hide nor hair of 'em. Maybe I can find some of the locals to help out. What do you make of that idea, Ty?" the marshal asked.

"Not a bad idea, but for me, I'd hold off for now. Bull-headed ranchers might lead to more problems you ain't no time for. Austin, you know this here territory better than just about anyone. These raids so far have been on the most vulnerable spreads, where things is set up giving a real edge to the raiders—especially in the dark. What is to keep you and me from putting ourselves in these fellows' boots? Start planning a raid of our own. Does that make a lick of sense to you?

The marshal stood at a window watching scattered snowflakes fall. They had begun to cover the boardwalks.

"Your run-of-the-mill lawman don't think like you, Ty. We should be taking the initiative instead of just reacting to them after the fact. I can come up with a handful of names right now. I sure can. It makes a heap of sense working at night, same as they done all along. Let's go down them lines tomorrow."

The two lawmen met the next morning for an early breakfast.

"I come up with four spreads, all with plenty of horses. Two is south of where the raiders done business first. Another is not too far away, toward Flat Creek Bottoms. The final one is Tim Thomas's place, due west of here, outside of Neosho Springs. Quite a sight, I have to say. It's almost impossible to find it the first time a man tries. Got lost myself. Finally just stumbled on it by pure luck. He's raising over a thousand head of cattle. Needs plenty of horses for all them beeves. Might be on them boys' list, 'cept he keeps some help around. They'd have to be extra careful. Diamond D hands is tough as nails."

"How far south is the first two spreads you got on that list?" Ty asked.

"No more than three hours ride to either. We could take a gander at both spreads tonight. They ain't very far apart. Then we could be back at your place before sunup."

"Makes sense, Marshal, with the snow letting up now and all. Word's been spread around now, so the bigger ranches are gonna be on the lookout for trouble."

It was a cold, clear night when the two lawmen paused in a small grove of snow-covered cedars, high above a ranch below. They carefully surveyed the layout below. "Ain't too big or too small, neither," the marshal remarked. "Fancied having a place like this myself someday." The ranch house was larger than most in the area. Smoke was streaming from two chimneys. A row of thick trees protected the northern exposure of the house. "I helped Nick put that barn up three years ago. We done it right, too, if I do say so myself. Nick Leslie is a real particular soul. Likes things just right. He and his boy runs things. Cattle's not as important as the horses he sells to the ranchers down this way. A square dealer, he does the bulk of horse business. Man's got a decent herd of longhorns, too. And that boy of his is one tough hombre. "

"Where are the horses, Marshal?"

"Ty, that's the thing that makes him a possible target in my mind. He keeps them damn near a mile from here, behind that flat hill you can see to the east. There's a fine shelter and real good fence amongst the cottonwoods down there where a small spring flows into a little creek. He keeps his cow dogs in at night, so unless there is one of his hands down there, a midnight raid would be very easy work. Nick's tight as a tick, so there ain't no hand around there until spring."

Later, after close inspection of the next ranch, Ty was in total agreement with the marshal's assessments. The full moon had allowed for good inspecting of all the spreads.

The following dark night, the two men led their horses down a steep incline behind a big house and adjacent red barn that was the Diamond D headquarters. A large outcropping of rock provided a clear view of all the outbuildings spread out in different directions. It was an impressive sight indeed.

"At first sight, I'm not seein' where this ranch is easy pickin's. Looks like both corrals is easy to see from anywhere around here," Ty said, looking through his field glasses. The clear night made for simple assessment of the setup.

"What a feller don't see makes me think of Tim's place. Most of his help don't stray there much, because they's triplets. They live just down the road a piece. The two hands that live in the bunkhouse is hard working, alright, but for the most part, they take to the jug at night. Tim don't seem to care. He's near blind from the war. Can't see a damn thing at night. Has to use a cane most of the time from getting shot up. It's a shame, too, for a young man like him. He can still run this fine spread though. If one of this bunch of thieves sees him hobbling around, it might get them thinking he is ripe for the pickin'."

"Sure enough," Ty agreed.

The night following the inspection of Nick Leslie's spread, they went to survey a tiny settlement. Bitter-cold north winds accompanied them on yet another clear night. Far below them sat a small, limestone ranch with a barn that dwarfed it. A stand of trees flanked a stream that was the northern boundary of the ranch.

"This here is the Bond place. A downright sturdy house. The brand has been in these parts a long time. Bar B ranch was one of the first out here in this grass. Real hardworkin' people, the Bonds. Got relatives all over this country. Keeps a fine remuda on the back side of that stream, to where it turns back towards the next pasture. It goes on well past his house and out of sight. Good for everything his horses require—'cept preventing thieves from taking them home with them. Course, he probably didn't think it would be much of a problem when the spread was laid out."

"Marshal," Ty announced. "Here's my two cents' worth of an opinion. Any of the spreads we see can be had for all different reasons. Any one of them for sure is fixing to be had, and soon."

"You ain't gonna git no argument from me, Ty. Any idea on where these horses is getting purchased?"

"Don't recall no horse thieves with this kind of appetite since I was a kid. They don't seem to be foolish, but they are going to have a serious problem moving these ponies from one place to another without being seen by somebody some time. You're telling me there's been sixty some confiscated so far which means, to my mind, they have to make a careful delivery of that size or more at night; that ain't easy. Two or three small parcels is not any safer.

Stopping to pack his pipe, the marshal pondered all the options. "That is for sure a big problem for them boys. Question is, what's a move we can make that makes sense? Do we try to find the horses hidden in these parts? Even if we found them, I guess they's got a dozen or more men in this bunch, so we would be no match if things got nasty. Plus, we'd have no backups we could count on."

"Thinkin' this delivery problem through, a man has to believe they might be forced to make one sometime soon. This here winter is not lookin' good. It's not a situation where sitting tight makes any sense. If it was me, I might just want to get rid of the horses before the weather made it impossible to do. We know for certain they won't be moving 'em south to Texas or Oklahoma. I'm leaning towards the north. Bad weather could be more of a problem if'n they wait much longer. Up there in Abilene, the railroad can move livestock in a hurry. Railroads east of here is too far to make any sense at all. I say we alert these spreads we seen, then tell all the ranchers to take special measures at night. It is all a guessing game, anyway. Maybe some luck will come our way, Austin."

"Horse thieves set my guts to churning. Ain't seen a one I wouldn't mind hanging," the frustrated marshal declared one more time.

Part Two

The Hunt

Help Arrives

Chapter 20

"My gambling instincts done me in," Ty said, over his third cup of coffee.

"Mine ain't no better, Ty. I was surprised as you was when they raided Tim Thomas's Diamond D spread."

Two weeks had gone by since the night visits to the most likely ranches. Weather-wise, the last week had been ideal for the raiders, with little visibility underneath the dark, cloudy nights. As a result, some thirty horses had disappeared.

"If these ranchers take things into their own hands, we will have more than we can handle," the marshal said gravely. Ty studied the troubled lawman's face. He saw desperation there.

"Says here we got some help coming. Picked my mail up last night and damned if my new friends from Dodge ain't coming to visit. Juan and his wife, Maria, are fixin' to find a place around here somewhere, and he's bringing an old buffalo soldier that was shot while I was on my way out here a ways back."

Ty handed the wrinkled letter to the surprised marshal. "Maybe the two of them will be looking for short-term work. If you don't have the budget that will allow you to pay them, I reckon I can handle it for awhile. They are both reliable men, and Juan done law work in the past."

"Well, that's a downright fine gesture, Ty. Damn if it ain't. I've got a little leeway since my deputy went to work for the Pinkertons. The letter says we could expect to see them in Tanglewood any day now. This development is pickin' up my spirits right now." Ty lit his smoke while the marshal went on. "If we was to gamble on future raids, what's your guess when this bunch of horse thieves might have to deliver to their buyer?"

"Soon," was Ty's quick response.

"Agreed."

"Where in your mind, Marshal, would you think them horses might be bound for?"

"Abilene. The railroad makes the most sense to me."

Ty agreed with a wry smile and a nod. "Tell you what else I believe, Marshal. If we had fifteen men, it could still take a month or more to find this outfit. With just two of us, it would be wasted time roamin' around, looking for a needle in a haystack. If we *were* lucky enough to find 'em what are you and I going to do about it? You and me need to keep an eye on the ranchers best we can before they add more trouble. *I* say, if I can convince my guests to join us for awhile, we make an effort to scout around Abilene for a big number of penned-up horses or maybe locate folks looking to buy some ponies in large quantities. I reckon these ranchers can give us good descriptions of some of the missing stock. It's time better spent, Marshal. Course it's up to *you* how you want to move forward."

"Let's give it a try. Hope we get the help you mentioned. Sure do."

Several days of rancher visits seemed to calm things down a bit. Good descriptions of some of the missing horses were noted, while the marshal assured the ranchers they had a plan that Ty, in particular, was in agreement with—not to mention that more help was expected anytime now.

Noon a day later brought Ty, along with two strangers, to the jail. One was a bulky, smiling black man. The other was a slight, bright-eyed Mexican wearing a broad sombrero. The marshal shook their hands enthusiastically. "Happy to meet you boys. Me and Ty got us a real problem. We could use some help, if you boys are so inclined."

"It would be our pleasure to be of assistance, Marshal. Roy turned his stables over to his best compadre. Then me and Maria decided it was time to vamoose to tallgrass country. Maria grew afraid in Dodge. Besides, if it's good country for the famous ranger Ty McCord, then me and Maria should be very happy here, too," Juan said excitedly.

Roy Johnson stood quietly by while his chatty friend went on talking. Ty noticed Roy seemed curious what his help might be needed for.

"You got trouble, I hear. What sort of trouble comes your way, Mr. McCord?" Roy asked.

"Me and the marshal are running a mite short on help. Seems the ranchers 'round here are missing more than a few horses. These raiders are real organized, with a big need for them rides. No doubt they got themselves a buyer somewhere. For our money, the buyer is in Abilene, where the railroad is handy," Ty replied.

Roy sat down in a large, rough chair next to the marshal. "Met ol' Ty out in Dodge when some crazies stole my money then set my stable on fire. Shot me, too, but not before I filled one of them with a dose of buckshot. The sheriff's boys found him the next day; he was in real bad shape. The others just abandoned him outside of town, so he was in a talkin' mood. Took two more days to round up the rest. They done been tried. Doin' time now."

"We got plenty of trouble here, but you boys can sure help. If'n we don't put an end to this thieving, the ranchers is going to go on a rampage and take matters into their own hands. We can't have that. Juan, Ty tells me you wore a badge in Texas and New Mexico. You of a mind to put one on in Kansas?"

Juan smiled broadly. "It would be my pleasure, Marshal, working with you and the famous ranger I met long ago. Ranger McCord delivered sweet justice to the men who killed my cousin Pedro."

"Count me in too, Marshal," Roy added. "Ty sure done me a real favor in Dodge."

Ty watched quietly while the men talked on with the marshal. His thoughts wandered between Liz and little DT and a plan of action to take the place of the guessing game that had led to nowhere. The addition of Juan and Roy raised the odds considerably in their favor. Ty could now set about a more aggressive approach. It was high time to hunt the thieves down. Even in the dead of night, it was strange that there had been no sightings of the raiders or their herd of stolen horses. In a twisted way, Ty admired their organized raids; these boys were clever. Finally, Ty joined the conversation.

"Austin, it might help if one of us goes to Abilene to take a look-see."

"Why not me?" Juan said. "Maria will not join me for a time. No one would know who I am in Abilene, so I can move around with mucho freedom. Maybe Juan will find someone who desires many horses."

"Fine idea! I'm figgerin' Abilene just *has* to be the delivery point—just as sure as I'm standing here. You go ahead, Juan. Be certain to locate the telegraph office as soon as you are able, so we can hear from you when necessary," the marshal said happily.

"Tomorrow, I will leave," Juan volunteered. "I will look for men with plenty pesos for purchase of so many horses. Juan will also seek where one might pen up such a number of animals. It takes plenty men for controlling them, too. Sometimes such hombres often will drink at night. Sometimes, too, they will let their tongue wag a bit too much. Juan will go about this work in Abilene, Marshal."

"Well, then, if you can make your way to Abilene tomorrow, I will be much obliged," the marshal added. "Be careful, and send me a report after meandering about. Take all the time necessary."

"Juan can do this. You will soon see. Buenas dias, Marshal Seward."

Confident Return

Sim Collin's mood had reached new heights. The second delivery of almost one hundred horses had exceeded every expectation. His idea of breaking up the trip into two separate groups, several hours apart, had worked to perfection. The pitch-black night had allowed them to go unnoticed, as far as he and his men could tell. The blustery winds and snow flurries combined to drive the inhabitants of their chosen route into their homes, close to the warmth of their fires. His riders had seen nothing whatsoever until they arrived at the deep-woods ranch.

Cole Clifford was pleased with the number and quality of the horses. He'd even consented to a price of ninety-nine dollars a head; this was two more dollars than the last delivery. It had been a payday like none Sim'd ever seen. His men, with the exception of Breed, had spent the night drinking and visiting Abilene whores without incident.

It was now mid day, with a brutal cold wind at their back as they journeyed back toward the hidden corral. So far, the railroad drop off was exceeding all expectations—quick, businesslike transactions. By the end of the coming year, Sim Collins was going to be a rich man, indeed.

As they progressed, Breed led the riders through a grove of snow-shrouded cedars then into a wide clearing surrounded by rolling hills in the distance. It was the halfway point on their return to the warmth of their carefully constructed shelters.

Sim noticed that the grumbling and taunting among his men had come to a halt. They had gained complete confidence in him; no fault was expressed about his decisions. He had clarity now about his future as a man of means. The decision to come to Kansas, although a gamble, had turned out to be a sage choice. The brand on his weather-beaten face would no longer be who Sim Collins was. His future tallgrass ranch, along with his fat bank account, would be his defining features; it seemed a near certainty. People would respect him as they did Cole Clifford. He would be a man to look up to. His future was surely *just* in front of him.

The long nights of the ruthless winter had helped guarantee their safe passage to and from Abilene. As they neared their hideout, he found himself supremely confident.

With the arrival of early spring, he would be altering his methods of delivery to account for the shorter nights that brought with them more danger of being discovered. For now, they would lay low, except for the necessary exceptions to gather supplies. A lone rider would go to a nearby settlement, scouting, on his way, for future prospects. Each and every rider was in agreement of Sim's plans. Even constant concerns about Breed and Peak had diminished considerably.

Juan's Reports

Juan's telegram was brief yet to the point: Abilene was
surrounded by many ranches. *That*, the marshal had
already known. But one in particular, owned by a certain
railroad baron, was not hospitable to strangers whatsoever. Saloon talk seemed to indicate the man had many
horses from time to time. More information could be
expected soon.

The marshal packed his pipe, pondering his situation. Something had to be done—and soon. To his way
of thinking, Abilene was cattle-and-railroad town. It was
also full of activity and with plenty of hombres with ques-
tionable pasts. It was Juan's understanding that the law
was inadequate and stretched to the limit in dealing with
drunk cowhands, general lawlessness, brawls, and occasional gunfights.

What the marshal now faced was tallgrass ranchers
who were very near to taking the law, or lack of it, into
their own hands. He had to convince himself, as well as the
angry ranchers, that he was going to put a stop to the raids.
He knew he was running short of time. Perhaps word of
Ty McCord's reluctant help would help in cooling them
off. Yet his window of time would close soon enough; the
ranchers would not hesitate to string up a suspected horse

thief at the drop of a hat. If that occurred, things would go to hell. It was a fine fix he was in.

A smiling Roy Johnson soon joined him at the jail. The old buffalo soldier always seemed to be in a good mood. "I'm takin' a downright likin' to this town. Sure am. Folks around here is real friendly, Marshal. Them hands at the Diamond D ranch is real fine people. They ask me to stay there as long as I want. Sonia Mae, she's the cook, can lay on a meal like I never seen. The boys say she came from Georgia after the war. Didn't see no woman in Dodge that was that pleasing to the eye, neither. You see, we've had conversations together. Ain't nothin' serious. She's a sweet little flower, though."

"Well, that's good, Roy. You ain't going soft on me, are you?"

"Don't plan to, Marshal. But I done fell for them collard greens and grits she's been servin'."

The marshal handed over Juan's wire for Roy to read. Putting it down on the desk, Roy asked, "How come you can't find a single soul that has set their eyes on a big bunch of horses being herded out of this grassland? Hardly seems possible; but then again, maybe the nasty winter was made for moving ponies."

"I been thinking the longer daylight is going to allow far fewer times to do just that. Wherever the horses are being taken, I expect these thieves are getting a damn good price. Otherwise, the risk of getting sent to the afterlife is just too great."

The next evening, the marshal received Juan's second wire. Juan somehow had come across a barkeep who was known to be connected with the grand railroad man, Cole Clifford. Van Dusen was the name. Juan suspected the barkeep was a man with an unsavory past. The man said Clifford was very private, except when he was being generous to the common folks of Abilene. Hardly anyone had set foot on his spread. He was known to buy horses.

The following weeks brought with them a consider-able number of Juan's wires. The sheriff in Abilene seemed to know little about Cole Clifford except some of his cowboys were tough hell-raisers prone to finding trouble in the saloons. Juan was to return to Tanglewood in a day or two. The marshal was anxious to visit with his talkative new friend. A few days after Juan's return, the marshal rode out to the McCord ranch.

"Well, Ty, I had a good long visit with Juan. I figger you have done the same these last few days. Here it is, the first day of May, with no reports of missing horses. Maybe them raiders moved on or are just letting things cool off a touch." The marshal leaned himself against the top rail of the big corral. "You sure done plenty of work on this place. That new peeled-pole gate is a real showstopper. Couldn't help but notice it when I come in."

"Thanks. Roy and I put in some time on it. I think it turned out fine myself. He and Juan are just down the road a bit. They been trying to outfish one another."

Eventually, all four men stood watching Ty's horses mill around his corral. Roy and Juan agreed with the marshal about the outstanding quality of Ty's remuda.

"That's as fine a bunch of ponies as I ever seen in one place."

"They ain't all broke yet," Ty said. "But it's time to talk about this horse-stealing business. We ought to all toss in our two cents' worth."

The lively powwow lasted until sundown. All had agreed it was unlikely the raiders had departed, due to the fact they had not been discovered; therefore, they wouldn't feel threatened. Next, Juan's trip to Abilene con-vinced them the stolen horses had to end up there. Cole Clifford was a likely buyer, with an isolated spread and a rank bunch of ranch hands. But no proof existed whatso-ever, and it appeared the law in Abilene kept their distance from Mr. Clifford.

"A few of these ranchers are about to bust a gut if I don't act. There is a rumor a vigilante committee is going to meet in a few days. No telling where and when," the agitated marshal said. "Raids of this type was supposed to have ended in '65. I wouldn't be surprised if they hire themselves a professional stock detective. Gunslingin' bounty hunters is all them detectives is. We sure don't need none of that!"

"The marshal and me noticed that the missing horses, at least ones we're sure of, seemed to all have been stolen south or west of here—that country between Florence and Cedar Point, then down to them spreads straddling the Walnut River." Ty stuck out both long arms in those directions to emphasize the statement. "Those big hills and long, tall flat tops, along with plenty of timber country, is ideal for holing up and staying out of sight. People is scarce as hen's teeth in all that space."

Ty fired up another long smoke then proceeded to wave his big forefinger in front of his face like an angry schoolmarm. "I made a lame gamble when we attempted to pick out the most likely ranches around here. We come up empty-handed then. Them raiders didn't hit a single one of those places we thought was ripe. Not one." The others nodded in agreement, somewhat surprised he was calling on so many words. "I'm putting more chips on the table. I'm bettin' these raiders are still out there somewhere, just biding their time. Fat and sassy. But they need supplies. Cattlemen are all on alert, so fetchin' food, whisky, horseshoes, and such ain't likely to be that easy. Making a commotion for supplies could be a mistake for them boys."

The marshal knocked back his hat on his forehead, then he pitched in. "In all that country, there's only three general stores between Florence, Green Ridge, and Burns. A man's got to do some serious traveling to find supplies in all that grass country. My chips is all in. Me and Ty figure it's time for us to pay a visit to all three towns. Be ready at sunrise."

Juan's next-day ride to Burns was accomplished on a rare windless morning. Burns sported one street with two structures on the east side and four on the west. Juan tied his horse to the rail in front of a sign that read *Lungren Blacksmith*. Oversized doors were held open by large, round barrels. Windows on both sides of the shop were open as well. Juan ambled through the doors to find the smithy seated on a stack of oak logs.

"Name's Hammer. That high-steppin' buckskin need shoein'?"

Juan shook the man's large, callused hand. "No, meester. I am Juan Jaramillo. Just passing through. The general store is closed, so I was wondering, perhaps, if you could tell me when it might be open for business."

"Don't rightly know, Juan. Whenever old Charlie is sober enough to stand upright, usually. Saturdays is good, but ain't no sure bet. Folks around here don't mind, though. He's our mayor, too, 'cause he ain't got no competition. I got a pot brewed. Care to join me?"

"Thank you, Meester Hammer. Sure could use a bit."

"Not much goes on here as a rule. Ranchers come by every three weeks or so. Banking is done somewhere else. We don't have no doctor, neither. I reckon I get my share of work, so I have no gripes. Strangers like yourself is rare. A while back, I did shoe as fine a looking dun gelding as I've seen in a coon's age. Had to come from fine stock somewhere. Can't say the same for the cowboy. He strutted down to the general store, found it closed. I told him same like I told you, but he went to see for himself. Came back mad as hell. Pitched a real fit. Wore a pair of low-slung Colt .44s. The man's spurs had them dangles on 'em! He jingle-jangled round here while I finished my work, then left in a flash. Good riddance, as far as I was concerned.

He wasn't up to no good at all. Worse yet, he had a face like a snake."

"Thank you for the information, Meester Hammer. Guess Juan needs to get back on the trail," Juan said, as he started to leave.

Hammer raised his bulging arms in protest. "I have to ask. You the law? 'Cause of all the horse thievin', I reckon the law was due to come sniffing around this country sooner or later. Juan smiled but didn't answer. "Don't matter to me one way or 'nother. Just askin'. You wouldn't be trailing that jingle-jangling rider, would you? I guess I was hoping you was. Strangest thing about that gelding of his was I noticed an ear marking. The left one had an 'H' behind it, just large enough to see. I been around horses all my life but never seen that before. I weren't born yesterday, neither. It don't mean nothing to nobody, no how. You come back and see old Hammer someday, compadre."

"Hasta la vista, Meester Hammer," Juan said, mounting his buckskin. He gently urged him north toward Green Ridge, where Ty would be waiting.

A Good Sign Raid

"Why don't you stop your bitching!" Sim said angrily. "You think I give a rat's ass that you are tired of cooling your heels? You'll do as I say—or else. A reckless man in our line of business is a liability. You ain't done your share of fetchin' supplies, neither!"

"Sit down, Peak." It was Zeb Hernandez who spoke up. "Them two ears on your head is for listening. Now's a good time to put them to use. We all have had enough of you beating your gums together. None of us like being holed up any more than you do. Keep in mind, you haven't been the featured guest at no necktie party, neither."

Jake Quinlan watched with a wry smile, along with the other riders, as Peak seated himself.

"As I was starting to say, we won't be here much longer. Too much daylight is our enemy. We all are aware of that. They's still plenty enough time to make one final delivery to Mr. Cole Clifford. Once we done that, I got an itch to buy a spread around here in the tallgrass. I'll be giving up our line of work. Course, there will be plenty of need for experienced hands once my herd is put together.

"Boss, you still got a price on your head," Dusty Nelson chimed in seriously.

"Not in Kansas," Sim snapped. "Listen up. Dusty,

give us your report from Green Ridge. Don't leave out nothin'."

Dusty came to his feet, looking around at all the riders.

"Whiles I was in the general store, there was several men jawing all about that spread up near Beezer. It is the same one I come upon some time back, when I was scouting in the evenings. They was saying that remuda had no equal in these parts. The ranch has a herd of over a thousand head and growing. One said the missus on that place was as fine looking as the remuda, so instead of coming here right away I went up there to take another gander. Well, they weren't tellin' no fish tale neither. I seen the missus working in her garden. Them horses in the corral was a sight for sore eyes. I left my horse behind some cedars a good quarter mile back so's I could get closer on foot. Took my field glasses along. A big darkie was working with the horses. There is nothing around that spread except waist-deep grass and hundreds of longhorns. Wasn't any way I could have been seen."

Sim leaned against the rough wall of the shelter. "You said something 'bout a picnic with some dancing was in the works for sometime soon?"

"You bet I did. It's set for June 26th."

Sim surveyed his men while Dusty talked.

"You figger to make a play on that remuda, Sim?" Jake Quinlan asked.

"Reckon so, Jake. I figger to make our last delivery our best. That spread should be a good place to hit while the hoedown doings is taking place. Before that we need to find fifty or sixty more horses that fit the bill for the delivery. Zeb got wind of a place not too far east of here that looks ripe for more horse business."

"Should be a safe place to start. While I was fetchin' some supplies, there was word in the store 'bout a funeral that was to take place two days from this here day. Man by the name of John Neihardt done passed. He was mighty old. He run one of the first spreads in these parts, but they were saying he had let the whole shebang go to hell," Zeb said. "Sounded like he weren't the neighborly type, neither. He run off all his help 'cept two worthless drunks. Cattle herd is down to nothing. One old boy spit out that he still kept a bunch of horses. Held onto them like they was his only real friends. Heard them saying, too, he was one of the early cowboys in the mid-sixties who drove those herds up from Rowenville, Texas, all the way to Sedalia, Missouri. Then they shut 'em down 'cause of disease. Supposed to have gunned a man down at Red River Station in '48. Come to Kansas pushing beeves up the Chisholm Trail."

"Zeb, you take Jake with you. Go sniff it out. Sounds like some of the talkin' might've been stretching the truth a shade," Sim ordered. "Do it tonight."

The men spent the remainder of the day tending the horses and engaging in various games of chance.

"Ripe as ripe can be," Jake said, upon their return at sunrise the next day.

Zeb added, "The place looks like the whole kit and caboodle is on the verge of caving in."

"Tomorrow, that codger goes in a hole in the ground," Sim said. "Midnight, then, is when we set them rides free. Any relatives that might be out there ain't going to be awake in the middle of the night, no how. Jed Els and Frank Leslie is in charge here while we do business."

Sim liked the fact his men took no liberty to complain when he was issuing his orders. Not even Peak. By the next day, threatening, dark clouds had gathered over a wide area. As the night grew, so did the dark-domed sky.

"Good sign," Breed said, while the men mounted up.

Rain had commenced before midnight and was coming down hard. Thunder boomed in the west behind them as Breed, Dusty, and Zeb led the way toward the dead man's treasured horses. As they proceeded, a herd of deer scurried ahead of them and scattered into the wet grass. A covey of quail flushed to the side of Peak's horse causing it to spook. All the riders noticed Peak reach for his Colt. Eventually, they came to a narrow-running creek. In the distance, the run-down fences of the Neihardt place began to take shape. A thick stand of cedars shielded the north border of the ramshackle little house.

Now sheets of rain obscured the riders. Breed opened the corral gate, allowing Dusty and Jake to ride into the midst of two dozen horses that began to circle the confines. Eventually, a stallion cleared the gate, followed by the remainder of the anxious group. Quickly, the riders herded them back through the rushing waters of the creek. Dusty and Breed rode close to the big stallion. The remaining men kept the followers in check until they clattered onto a trail leading to the safety of the hideout. Sim trailed his men, along with a lone straggler he had roped. The little zebra dun was snubbed to his saddle horn.

The raid had gone down without a hitch. Later, alone inside his rough shelter, Sim pondered what was to lie ahead. He told himself he was no fool; therefore, it was natural for the ease of the night's raid, aided by the heavy rain and black sky, to drum up some uneasiness. Luck had been his sidekick, but would it hold out on him when he needed it the most? For now, his riders were held in check. Most were dangerous, wild men, hungry for the spoils of their brazen raids. In some, the loyalty wasn't near hide deep. Sim didn't intend to push his good fortune past the final transactions in Abilene. He cottoned to no man but himself. It didn't pay.

The flawless raid began to bring on a brooding state of mind that gnawed at him like a starved rat. His sleeplessness was trailed by a damp, chilly morning. Silently, he watched his men examine the Neihardt remuda, wondering how much time would pass before someone would notice the empty corral. Prancing and moving about nervously, the horses suspiciously took stock of their new owners as well. Sim rubbed his rough chin as Zeb approached. "That old codger may have let his spread go to hell in a handbasket, but I tell you straight, Sim, them rides is all been taken fine care of."

"So I seen," Sim agreed.

"The boys—and even *Breed*—ain't seen no better since we arrived here in Kansas. They are a top-dollar find."

Sim's dark mood hung on throughout the morning. Rain returned by mid-day, bringing along a strong, penetrating wind that drove the riders to shelter. Silence fell over the hideout. Sim's thoughts retreated to the deadly episode in Raton, New Mexico. It had been a day like this one when things went bad. His two unreconstructed outlaws had handled themselves well during the bank holdup. Desperate for the money, he had taken an unwise risk with the two men. Clear of Raton that morning, the good-fortune suspicions of a perfect heist had begun to invade his brain. They had stopped in a clearing long enough to water the horses. His saddlebags held the money—all seventeen thousand of it. There had been few words exchanged during their getaway. Tall and almost toothless, the outlaw from Round Rock had remarked that he was proud it had not been necessary for gunplay in Raton. Killings always riled the townsfolk. Sim agreed, noticing Lanky's Colt was hanging loose. Smaller and younger, the other outlaw had seemed noticeably fidgety. The only name he went by was Luther. A light rain had begun to fall when Lanky had suggested it was as good a time as any to divide up the money. Luther stood near the rocky creek, shifting from one foot to the other, tossing loose stones into the water.

Then, without warning, Lanky drew his pistol, shooting his unsuspecting companion in the chest and knocking him spread-eagle backward into the water. In an instant, his Colt held Sim at bay. "I'm figuring we best split that money up right now. That boy was just a liability, as far as I was concerned. Couldn't be trusted, no how. Just pull that sack slowly out of your saddlebag."

Sim remembered Lanky's foul breath when he had stepped close to his horse. Carefully, the money sack was pulled out while Sim locked his angry eyes on Lanky's own sunken, undersized, and beady pair. Sim's left hand held the sack securely in front of him, shielding the Smith and Wesson pocket .32 he held in his right. Reaching for the money, Lanky lowered his pistol ever so slightly—a total mistake it had been. Sim recalled the look on Lanky's face when he had delivered two deadly shots to the outlaw's broad forehead.

Cole Clifford's money combined with the hidden seventeen thousand from Raton would indeed buy him a fine tallgrass spread. That day was nearing. By sundown, Sim's dark mood finally gave way to welcome plans of another new raid.

Green Ridge Decisions

"Amigos," shouted Juan, as he trotted up to the only commercial structure in sight. Roy, along with Ty, noted the excitement in his cheery, high-pitched voice. "I, Marshal, bring good news!" he exclaimed, jumping down from his buckskin. "Meester Hammer, the blacksmith, well, he's seen a pony that had been earmarked. Noticed it behind his left ear. Told Juan it was a small 'H'. His rider was intent on visiting the closed general store that was only sometimes open for citizens and visitors."

"Was the man who rode that pony into Burns familiar to this Hammer fellow?" the marshal asked seriously.

"No sir, Marshal. He said he had never set eyes on him before. He said to me that he wore jingle-bobs on his spurs. Strutted like a banty rooster, with a face that reminded him of a snake. A no-good hombre was Meester Hammer's take."

"Well, then, an old soldier like me, who ain't all that smart, knowed the thieves is most likely to be around here somewheres. That horse come from the Hogan ranch, sure as I am standing on this dirt."

"Reckon that's right, Roy, but we ain't sure 'til we locate them slippery thieves," the marshal remarked, removing his pipe from his stained teeth.

"A man's gotta believe they'd only hang around these parts for one reason. We all know what that means," said Ty.

"That store in Florence was a bustling place when I arrived," Roy went on eagerly. "The woman ramroddin' the store never stopped talking. Didn't matter none who it was, neither. Finally, I was able to get a word or two in edgewise. I inquired regarding new faces in the store. She looked at me kinda funny like. Then she said that besides me, there were only two others. I gathered they come in on two occasions. Both times, the men came together, taking with them a heap of supplies. Just when I was fixing to leave, she remembered the fine horses they was riding."

"As far as I was concerned, here in Green Ridge, the folks that stopped in said word had spread around about our place in Beezer. A while back, a feller had come in to fetch some flour, coffee, and salt. Told the owner here he had passed by my place a time or two. He didn't offer up no name. Nobody seemed to recognize him, neither."

"Ain't no mystery, Ty, that spread of yours is getting a deserved reputation."

"I'll admit, Marshal, that it's coming around right nice. I'll be needing another hand right soon. Juan, Roy, and me won't cut it this spring; too damn much to do with all them new calves. Ben sent me a letter just this past week. Says he'll be arriving mid-May sometime. That will help, but his lumbago is giving him fits. He ain't exactly no spring chicken."

Presently, Juan and Roy disappeared inside the little store in search of ammunition and other supplies.

Ty lit a smoke. "I get the drift of your thinking, Austin. I suppose my place could be a destination for this band of thieves, except for the obvious fact that Beezer is a long ride from a direct trail to Abilene."

"True enough I reckon, Ty. But I have a notion you

already had given a bit of thinking to the possibility of a raid."

"You ain't totally barking up the wrong tree, Marshal. One way or another, I'm feeling a mite better about our gamble."

"I no longer doubt those riders is still somewhere in all that space. As these fine, warm, long days come on, the nights ain't gonna be their ally, like it was in the winter months."

"You ain't gittin' no argument from this direction. Seems Green Ridge and Florence is more reliable for re-supplying. The odds of one of us being in either town when the strangers return is downright slim. Course, there ain't any other law to help out. That leaves us with the likelihood of another raid, and the ranchers taking the law into their own hands. Ty, the best bet, seems to me, would likely be conjurin' up a scheme to make these varmints come to us."

"I said before, Austin, you have my word. The thieving has to stop. I have wondered when you was just going to lay your plan out and stop hemmin' and hawin' about it. Why don't you just come right out and get it over with? It's my ranch that is going to be bait, with my remuda being the prize. Truth be told, I considered it myself, figuring the outcome might be in my hands. What's been holding me up is breaking it to Liz. She ain't about to agree to no fool plan, not to mention the holy hell she'll likely raise. Controlling that stallion of mine is a downright picnic compared to Liz."

"That sorta brings to mind my other idea you ain't con-sidered, most likely."

Roy and Juan appeared again, carrying supplies. The marshal tapped his pipe on the rail then relit it yet another time.

"You fancy horse racin', boys? Well, I can't recall the last time there was one around Beezer, so I'm proposing one be set up for the first day in June. I believe that's a Saturday. Let's hear what you men make of the idea."

"To my way of thinking that would be a real fine way to spend a day, Marshal," Roy piped in.

Juan slapped his thigh, showing a wide smile. "My Maria will be here in time. Mucho happy will she be when she finds out!"

Ty fingered the brim of his hat, heeling the last of his smoke in the dirt. "Fine thinking, Austin. Strangers come from just about anywhere for a good race. As a rule, the horses get all the attention. Most folks don't care much about a body they ain't seen before. Exactly where you figgerin' it ought to be run, Marshal?"

"Thought it over last evenin'. That parcel just a ways north of Sharp Creek is flat as a pancake. There'd be plenty of space to handle quite a few watchers."

"No place around is better for a race," Ty agreed. "Naturally, it happens to be less than a mile from my place. Liz is gonna throw me plumb out of the house. She ain't about to take this sittin' down—you know that, Marshal, don't you?"

"Reckon I do."

"If there ever was a way to draw them riders out in the open, this orta be a good bet. Not only will my remuda be close at hand, but they can easily take a gander at the Bellemere and Mehrer spreads. Then, too, a man could move about here and there without much attention paid to 'im."

"Ty, my old mind was heading down that same path," the marshal said proudly.

Chapter 25

Sim's Luck Holds

Almost a month had passed, with each day growing progressively longer, before Dusty and Zeb confronted Sim. Zeb took the lead in the conversation.

"Boss, me and Dusty got a need to discuss this here situation."

"Well, spit it out, Zeb. I'm in no mood for no long-winded speech. Make it short and sweet."

Zeb toed the stones at his feet. It was a rare windless day. A few minutes went by.

"The entire outfit is getting a mite edgy. Damn near the entire month passed by whilst we been hunkered down. Fights have broken out three times in the last week. It's getting real hot out here, too. We're all questioning why we ain't stole more rides."

Sim was leaning against a sizeable locust tree, avoiding the mid-day sun. "You boys think I ain't paying attention to what's going on 'round here?" he growled. "You said nothing that I ain't aware of. Truth be known, I'm just waiting on some weather. Breed come to me two days ago with an idea, so me and that young deserter we picked up in the Nation went callin' last night. It's a two-hour ride. They's showing enough horses to fill out one half what I'm figgerin' on delivering to our upstanding Mr. Clifford.

Breed's night wanderings is constant, we all know. Says he has scouted the place three times. Seems a woman with two young men is living on the place. Right nice bunch of horses is penned up a good quarter of a mile from the house. Breed don't lie none."

"This will be music to the ears of the men," Dusty said happily, as he left to spread the news.

"Somethin' new just come up when we picked up our supplies," Zeb said.

"Tell me about it quick, then."

"There is wild news! Notices is posted in the stores telling about a big horse race planned for the first day of June. Them announcements is plastered everywhere."

"I ain't heard about it," Sim acknowledged.

"Well, the boys is throwin' around the topic among themselves."

"Where?"

"Just outside of Beezer. They's competing for a thousand dollars! It's billed out as the biggest race ever held in tallgrass country. Rumor is them notices has been posted for miles in all directions. A big crowd is expected no doubt."

"We kinda figured that daylight scoutin' for our final delivery wouldn't raise suspicions none with the ranchers. The races gonna occupy most people's attention."

Sim shoved his stained hat to the side of his half-bald head. The ugly brand on his face stood out in the bright sunshine. Zeb tried to avoid staring at it. His eyes sought the safety of his worn boots while he waited for Sim's reaction.

"Dusty and you, Zeb, is dependable as I got in this here outfit. Yessiree, that's how I see it. I never had no reason to doubt you straight shooters. If'n this next night run, whenever it is, don't stir up trouble for us, then I reckon some of the boys might just attend them races. Fact is, I might just go with 'em."

"Breed volunteered to remain with the horses. Two others ain't interested in the races none. Won't be nothing to worry about while the rest of the outfit is away," Zeb assured before hurrying away.

Six days passed by before a dark and moonless night sent the riders toward the horses in the tallgrass two hours south. Eventually, they gathered in a crowded stand of cottonwoods and thickets within view of the penned-up horses. Sounds of the owls and the wild chirping of other birds accompanied the gang while they bided their time. Coyotes in the distance howled into the darkness. Their horses held tight to the cover, only shivering and swatting away at the insects with their tails. Eventually, Breed's horse slipped quietly from the safety of the trees. Breed walked beside her. A dark-colored shoulder blanket made him next to invisible in the high, thick grass. He had shed his hat. His long hair was as black as the night. Within a very few steps, only the horse was visible as they advanced slowly toward their prey.

Suddenly, the woman Breed had seen when scouting the spread came running wildly toward the horses. Her hair was flying, and her arms were flailing in the dark. The hidden riders watched as a laughing, yelling man ran behind her. A gun was in his hand. Whispering, the men noticed Breed's horse was out of sight, too. Dusty remembered Breed had confided once to him that his horse could kneel on command. The running man was closing the gap between him and the woman. "I will have you tonight, you bitch!" he laughed evilly. "So you best stop, as I will be forced to shoot those pretty legs of yours. Don't think I won't. Don't make me do it, bitch!" The man laughed some more. Now he was within arm's length.

The woman's cries rang out when she stumbled. He stood over her prone, exhausted body with his pistol still drawn. Sim's riders glanced back and forth at each other.

Night-adjusted eyes made out a handful of clothing he held over his head. Now it appeared he was struggling with his trousers and trying to keep the six-shooter at the ready all at once.

Peak spoke up, "The son of a bitch is drunk as a skunk. He sure as hell gonna have hisself a time if he don't pass out."

"That's enough, Peak," Sim ordered.

Jake and Zeb just looked annoyed. Then all talk ended abruptly. Standing behind the laughing man was a dark silhouette that unmistakably belonged to Breed. The robe still covered his shoulders and back, giving him the image of a statue in the grass. The man was unaware of his presence until a strong hand grasped his chin, forcing it skyward. The silent riders watched as Breed's pig sticker rendered the man silent forever.

Sim watched, and the sneer on his face grew. Urging his horse next to Peak's, he spoke so all his men could hear. "You go near that woman, Peak, and I'll have Jake horsewhip you with that lead-tipped rawhide rig of his." Peak looked around at the riders, finding only blank faces.

"Them horses is waiting to be stole. Let's finish the job," Dusty declared, emerging from the dark.

"Dusty," Sim growled. "You find out about the woman. I see Breed's already inside the pen. I'll deal with that situation."

The breathless young woman was on her back, staring at the star-vacant sky, when Dusty approached her. She tried to speak, but the words refused to surface. She had wrapped herself in Breed's buckskin robe. The laughing man was bleeding out, beside her yet she didn't seem to notice his lifeless body. Her unblinking eyes stared at Dusty's night-shrouded face. Presently, he walked away, mounted his horse, and rode into the night among the stolen horses and Sim's anxious riders.

Breed was unaccounted for. The reluctant horses were

pressed on in the darkness by the men. Sim made sure Peak was among them. Dusty alertly rode beside Sim.

"She weren't hurt none," Dusty reported. "The woman, I mean. Scared speechless. Breed must a put his blanket around her then opened the pen. I don't want no trouble with the silent one ever."

Breed rode into the hideout wearing his buckskin blanket the second night following the raid. Emotionless and silent, he slid down his horse, oblivious of eyes following him.

Sometime later, Sim found Breed alone near the concealed entrance to the hideout. "You didn't have no need to kill him, Breed," Sim said angrily. "Someone is bound to find him missing. That will mean trouble. Trouble is what we don't need. Business has been goin' just fine, then you take the unexpected matters in your own hands."

"Breed don't worry none about dead, bad man. Wolves found him in the wallow where I put the body. Bones is mighty hard to make sense of once the varmints has finished their work."

Eventually Sim sauntered away, thinking that it wasn't Breed that had riled him up. Perhaps it was the good fortune that was certain to run its course at a time unknown to him.

Within the week following the dark night events, the prairie became shrouded under persistent, dark gray, menacing clouds. Another night raid was accomplished without detection.

Race Bait

"From the looks a things, tomorrow is gonna find more people in Beezer than the locals ever dared to imagine," the marshal revealed, while pouring Ty a generous cup of steaming coffee. "Even the telegraph office is swamped. When banker Wendling come through with a thousand dollars in prizes, word musta spread like a wildfire. Hell, an aunt of mine even wired me about the doings. That's the only word I've had from her in a coon's age. Juan told me last evening the smithy, Hammer, he talked to in Burns is coming. Bringing his grandson along with him, too."

Ty stared into his coffee, "Sounds right promising. You make any progress with them ranchers?"

"I mighta, but ain't no tellin'. Come down from the saloon boiling mad. Mostly whiskey talk, though. None of them have had horses taken, neither. They made it damn clear hiring gun-handy cowhands is an idea being tossed around, too. If I read 'em right, I truly think some among them picked up a bad case of horse-race fever. Every last one was gonna have a horse entered. Just maybe we bought us a tad more time to deal with them thieves."

"Hope that turns out to be the situation," Ty remarked.

"How'd it go with Liz? You did tell her your remuda was bait, didn't you?"

"'Course I did, Austin. I ain't *that* afraid of her tantrums." A broad smile took shape on the marshal's worn, angular face.

"How long did the hemmin' and hawin' go on before you come out with the plan?"

"I bided my time. Didn't rush nothin'. Enjoyed myself some whiskey. Following my third cup, them words come rolling out real smooth like. That was when she commenced to callin' me some names that I recall being unpleasant. You wasn't mentioned with no respect neither, Marshal."

"No way I'm surprised with that report. To my way of thinkin', you ain't afraid of much of anything, with the lone exception of Liz McCord."

"I reckon I ain't in no position to deny it. When that woman gets her dander up, she scares the holy hell out of me. If'n it wasn't for Ben McCullough, I'da been in for even more of a tongue-lashing. He come knocking on our door 'bout when Liz was fixing to raise the roof right off the house."

The marshal tended to his ever-present pipe, then poured Ty another cup. "Seems a little strange you ain't mentioned nothing about entering that gray beast of yours in this here contest.

"You and Juan is in cahoots over racin' Grey, ain't you?"

The marshal lit a match under the desktop then put it to his pipe. "Guilty as charged, Ty. That rascal has been in this place more times than you can imagine. Wants to get on that stallion so damn bad he can taste it. Makes a right solid case, too. I reckon size-wise, he's about half the load you would be. Personally, gamblin' ain't something I cotton to, as a rule, but if he were to run, I might consider a wager or two, should the occasion arise."

"Grey ain't carried nobody but me, Austin. Why, he'd just as soon toss that little devil sky-high than look at him, unless I spent the better part of my day with him and Juan.

Grey ain't a whole lot different than Liz when it comes to agreeing to ideas that ain't exactly his own."

"You ain't afraid of losin' are ya, Ty?" the marshal added comically.

"Now, Austin, you could of left them words in your gullet where they come from. This is what I'll agree to, but nothin' else: you find that little Mexican and tell him to be at my corral by high noon today."

"It will be my pleasure, Ty. Damned if it won't be."

Ty found Liz, little Darren, and Ben on the porch when he trotted into the yard. Grey was led into the barn, then Ty joined everyone on the porch.

"We been jabbering about the place. You picked a fine spread, any way a fellow looks at it. I reckon I never set these old eyes on so much tallgrass in my life," Ben said happily.

"Wasn't no way to make it all happen without your money. I'm much obliged to you," Ty said honestly, glancing toward Liz, who offered a reluctant smile.

"That ain't all, Ty," Ben went on. "Meeting Liz has been a downright pleasure, and little Ty is quiet as a church mouse."

Liz piped up, "Takes after his daddy."

"Them's true words, Liz, but the little feller's got a strong resemblance to *you*. Seems to me he's a mite better off for it, too. No offense, Ty."

"I ain't taking none, Ben."

When the conversation turned to the recent spring roundup and the races, Liz took little Ty and sought the confines of the house.

"As far as I'm concerned, the plan you and the marshal has conjured up just might work," Ben stated, while enjoying his lemonade. "I think it's just plain horse sense to assume if them thieves is enjoying trouble-free stealing, then they more than likely is gonna stay put. If they is in the crowd and get a close eyeful of them ponies of yours, it's goin' to set them off to licking their lips at the thought of making off with the whole lot. They shot Millie Hogan, and I can't get the sight of her dyin' out of my mind. *Praying*, I am— hoping to high heaven they step in the snare."

"Me and the marshal is expecting a heap of trouble with the ranchers around here if this don't work," Ty admitted.

"Them brazen killers need to swing in the wind, Ty," Ben said adamantly. "I'll be staying around this place while the race is happening. Gawkers near the corral is what 'ol Ben here is going to be watching closely. There was a time when I convinced myself little Ty was helping overtake the pain of Millie Hogan's brutal death. If the races bring them out in the crowd, your remuda will draw them near, like flies to raw meat. Seems to me they wouldn't attempt no raid real soon," he speculated. "Time would be needed for the ideal conditions to develop. No matter though, one foot would have already stepped in the snare."

Ty McCord was simply the most dangerous man Ben had ever witnessed in dealing with the worst of the unde- sirable elements on the frontier. Kansas was young. It drew the bold, unruly individuals with unsavory practices right along with those that simply desired a new life. Justice was delivered mightily to those who chose to steal a man's horse: criminals that committed murder often escaped the hangman's noose; horse thieves rarely were spared. Those who trafficked in horseflesh had to be careful. Open-range horses were the ranchers' conveyance, yet even the most upright among them had no reservations to a few whole- some hangings. Although Ty now sought a different exis- tence, he had found he wasn't able to completely escape his considerable reputation that had ridden beside him into the tallgrass. For some men, the past refused to leave them alone; Ty was one of those men. Horse thieving was running wild. All signs seem to confirm they had another hand to play. The age-old magnetic effect of exceptional horses could cause even the most cautious of men to lose track of their senses.

Lost in his thoughts, Ben was slow to react to the large, muscular man approaching. His horse was already snubbed to the rail.

"Name's Lundgren. Most folks call me Hammer. I take it this here's the McCord ranch."

"Indeed," Ben answered.

"I come here for them races. Looking for a little Mex, too. Calls himself Juan Jaramillo. Met him awhile back. Talkative little feller."

"Well, you come to the right place. Juan is in that pasture behind this here house, trying his best to stay on top of a big, gray stallion he claims he can ride tomorrow," Ben revealed.

"I never seen these parts of Kansas with so many horse-crazy folks. Trails is plumb full of buggies and such headed this way. They's even come with tents. Got some set up in the grass not far from here. The town's overflowing. Peddlers is thick as fleas on a cur dog."

"Juan told me you seen an earmarked pony out your way. I reckon being a smithy and all, it's a natural curiosity that keeps your job interesting. I was a lawman down in Oklahoma, so I was familiar with them thieves, particularly in the Cherokee Nation. Don't ever recall but one spread that done ear markings. Only on the finest horseflesh did they up and mark 'em. The place was outside of Guyman. The MH ranch was huge with over five thousand head of longhorns. No place in these parts could compare with the MH when it come to raising horses, neither. Some were thoroughbreds like I never seen before or since."

Hammer rummaged through his shirt pocket, retrieving a half-smoked, thick cigar and relighting it. "I won't soon forget that dun with the black mane and tail. He was something to look at for damn sure. I didn't have no appreciations for the rider though. Reminded me, some, of them camera pictures I seen of Emmitt Dalton before they put him away for good. Right nasty-looking cowboy. That feller didn't have no business on that horse."

"Well, I tell you one thing's for damn sure: that horse belonged to Millie Hogan," Ben said grimly. "Whoever pulled that raid off killed Millie while they was at it. Horse thieving and murder; it don't get no worse than that, mister."

"You reckon that is the same bunch that's been doin' the stealin' in these parts?"

"Makes sense to *this* old lawman. They ain't been bothered yet. To my way of reasonin', they is sitting pretty in this here grass, being the law is stretched to the limit out here. But you mark my words, Mr. Hammer: things is fixin' to change. Something tells me they's gotta be powerful tempted by the goings on tomorrow. If they *are* in the crowd that traipses past Ty's remuda, it's gonna set their heads to spinning. There is a lot ridin' on that being the case. 'Course, I could be barking up the wrong tree, but I don't think so."

Luck-Broke

An uncommon east wind softly blew open the cloudless morning. In the field behind the tack room, a doe and her fawn were spirited through the waving grass by a large, energetic, black dog. Eventually, Hammer emerged from its confines, proceeding to wash up in a large wooden bucket.

"A man couldn't expect no better day for a race," Ben said, as he walked toward the big smithy. "I brung you some of Liz's coffee. Ain't tasted much better myself. She's got them griddle cakes stacked on the stove inside, too. Kinda figured you might have an interest."

"I don't never turn down the opportunity, Ben. You bet I do. Nothing I like better," the happy smithy answered.

"Once you have your fill, the marshal and Ty are wanting to have a powwow before this thing kicks off," Ben revealed seriously. "Marshal says there's a report about a killing and more missing ponies a ways south of here."

"Don't that beat all, now!" Hammer said as he dried his broad face. "Them boys is sure pressing their luck. I'd like to do something to help, but I ain't much good in the dead of night, to tell you the truth."

"That makes two of us, but you got that careful,

close-up eye. Marshal says he would like to take advantage of that there leanin'."

"Count me in, then. My whole town is vacant anyways, 'cause of these here races. I can stay an extra day or two if needed."

Shortly, while the sun continued to rise, Ty and the marshal laid out the roles of the men for the day. Not far from where they sat, dozens of grassland inhabitants began to stream by.

"Since you're game, Hammer, we could sure use you to be on the lookout for fine horseflesh here and there, if you get my drift," the marshal said. "Ben is sitting tight right here, watching for lingering gawkers 'round this here place."

Ty sat quietly enjoying his coffee and smoke while the marshal laid out the all-in gamble.

"I hear up to seven or eight hundred folks will be milling 'round this ranch, going and coming to the races. This morning, I seen gypsy photographers selling them pictures for fifty cents. I never seen the likes of this in the tallgrass. If them thieving bastards ain't in *this* crowd, they's the only ones that ain't. Why, even old Doc Deiderich is takin' the afternoon off, unless some damn fool breaks his neck in the races."

Finally, Ty got up from his chair and lit another smoke. "It's time to join the crowd at the track. You folks carry on with whatever you are supposed to be doin'. I can't wait to watch Juan try to stay on top of Grey in front of all these visitors."

The third race had just concluded when Ty arrived at the track; he was amazed at what he saw. Most of several counties' inhabitants surely were in attendance. A brisk, steady wind was sweeping over the happy visitors. Enterprising men and women were hawking candy, lemonade, photos, baked goods, and even straw hats. Bets were being placed at both ends of the racetrack, along with printed lists of horses and riders. Prominent citizens in their finery looked on from their buggies. Frolicking children seemed to be everywhere, closely followed by anxious, young mothers.

The track was surrounded with deep-seated fence posts and heavy rope. In the center was a circular wooden stand that held the judges. Sitting proudly was banker Wendling along with Doc Dietrich and the mayor, who had proven himself to be the most incompetent individual for miles around. The scene exceeded anything Ty might have imagined. No self-respecting horse thief would be able to resist this kind of temptation; he might think his attendance carried no risk at all. Besides, no one knew most of the crowd, only their closest neighbors along with a handful of prominents. A thief might be standing by or talking to those he may have helped relieve of their precious horses. The races surely would draw them out in the open, sensing no threat whatsoever.

Ty and the Marshal's bet could just prove to be a solid gamble. Besides, the marshal and he had run their options out if the thieves didn't take the bait. All hell was about to break loose in the very near future, and the two of them stood to be surefire recipients of the grassland ranchers' wrath.

Sauntering through the noisy, happy visitors, Ty made a point to stop and place a bet on the next race. Forty or fifty rough-hewn cowboys were placing bets among themselves, as well. The beer was fueling the noise level of the gamblers' conversations. Ty wondered if any of them were night riders in the tallgrass, riders that were not only thieves and killers but were also boiling the blood of the ranchers. Presently, the next race bolted ahead at the sound of a shot from the mayor, a man Ty had come to like despite his shortcomings.

Big Roy Johnson joined Ty. With him was a slim, middle-aged black woman. She seemed to have inherited

Roy's ever present smile. "This here's Sonia Mae. Might you remember I done told awhile back that she's up from Georgia," Roy announced proudly.

She was wearing a bonnet and a long, bright, multicolored dress. "Ever since Roy's been staying at the Diamond D, we been friends. I suppose he likes my cooking some."

Ty suspected that wasn't the only thing the big man had come to enjoy about the comely woman. Easy to look at, with bright, intelligent eyes, Sonia Mae had hogtied Roy for certain. "My people was born and raised just outside of Macon, Georgia. I followed my brother after he arrived through the Underground Railroad."

"A pleasure meeting you, Sonia Mae," Ty said, as the happy duo departed.

Minutes later, Ty found the smithy standing near the finish line. A stub of a dark cigar protracted from his teeth. Around him, some bettors were discussing the outcome of the last race. Hammer was waving the dust away from his face with his well-worn hat.

"Ain't this something, Ty," he said excitedly when Ty approached. "In all my born days, this beats all I ever seen. Plenty of menfolks I seen is bearing sidearms. Must be riled up over all the theivin' that's beset 'em. I reckon I could be wrong, though."

"No you ain't seein' crooked, Hammer. Me and the marshal seen it going on for a time now. We are more than a touch troubled all hell is fixing to bust out soon," Ty responded gloomily. "Say, why don't we catch onto a cold beer off that wagon yonder."

"I could surely use one about now, Ty. Besides, I got some information that you might favor."

Ty's heartbeat quickened as they seated themselves under a nearby locust tree. Hammer's expression alerted him to a possible breakthrough of some sort. Hammer took a long, welcome swig of his beer, then he commenced to relight the stub of his cigar. "Being partial to good horses like I am, I wandered over in that grove of cottonwoods over yonder that's all shady and nice. Plenty of horses to look at, that's for sure. It's just far enough from the track. Seems like there wouldn't no prying eyes—especially with the runnin' going on."

Ty found a long cheroot in his breast pocket and fired it. Anticipation was building now, as Hammer was carefully choosing his slow-traveling words. "You being a ranger of reputation, I want you to know my young days was filled with things I ought not to have done. But the war changed me for the better, if a body can believe that. Never was a wanted man or nothing, though. I have finally smoked the peace pipe—with my past." He paused to consider this then continued. "Don't rightly know why I jabbered on about those days, less'n maybe I thought you would find me lacking trust. I got some making up to do in my life."

"We all got regrets, Hammer. I never met no rangers neither that was anywheres near to being a saint."

Two young girls skipped past them, squealing with delight as they went on their merry way.

"Best you get on with what you seen in them cotton-woods and cedars."

"What I seen was a passel of well-bred rides. Among them was two geldings and a little filly, all earmarked with Millie Hogan's 'H,'" Hammer said excitedly, waving his cigar in front of his wind-burned nose. "'Course, it don't mean the thieves rode them there at all, does it? Coulda been anybody, I suppose. It come to my mind we might watch close to eye who rides out with 'em. Well, then I seen Roy and Sonia Mae samplin' some of them baked goods. They hollered at me to join them for a taste of them cakes and such. When I come back I couldn't believe them Hogan horses had done vamoosed. Damn it, Ty, I should have never left. I feel downright horrible. Fit to be tied, I was." Ty listened with heightened interest as Hammer kept talking. "I swear I had lost every race I wagered on, then the horses disappear! I was plumb luck-broke! Then Lady Luck done a switch back on me. Stomping mad, I made tracks for the beer wagon. Then I up and seen him."

"Who was it?"

"It was that snake-faced bastard who come to get his gelding shoed at my place over at Burns. I noticed he was still wearing them jingle-bob spurs, too, and running his mouth. He was complaining to high heaven 'bout his bets was rotten. That Hogan horse he was riding that day was fine, you'll recall. I mentioned it awhile back."

"I do recall. A dun with a black mane and tail, if I ain't mistaken."

"That's right, Ty. You remember good." Hammer replied. "So I kind of moved away in the crowd but close enough to eyeball him. Next thing I know, three other men come looking for him. Then they commenced to convince him to come with them. Seemed like they was in a hurry to go somewheres, so I followed 'em. They didn't see me, 'cause they was talking up a storm. Didn't seem they was too happy with that drunk snake-face. They walked toward the creek just down the hill over yonder." Hammer pointed the direction with his cigar, wide-eyed with excitement. "Got just close enough to spot jingle-bobs's dun and the same Hogan horses that was snubbed in the cottonwoods. Once they saddled up, they was slow-trotting in the direction of your spread. Didn't seem to be in no hurry. Lots of folks were on the road and splashing around the creek. They didn't seem to notice anyone, either, from what I seen. High-dollar horses like them Hogans don't come cheap—unless you're a thieving killer."

"Let's go find the marshal. We just might have to miss the last race, even though Grey is the favorite. This here situation is a damn sight more important. My spirits is a mite bit better than they have been, then, thanks to you, Hammer."

The prairie had begun to cloud over a bit, and the

house had taken on a coolness that greeted Hammer and Ty as they stepped inside. They found Ben sitting there with the marshal.

"You ain't going to watch Grey run?" Ben asked, surprised at seeing Ty.

"Nope. I already know how fast he is. Doubt he's prone to lose. Guess it's possible but ain't likely. Hammer here seen four Hogan horses up close. That's how come we are here instead of there."

"Well, now. We're all ears," the marshal said excitedly.

Ty had begun to sense an old familiar doggedness about the possibilities before the men. All of them listened carefully as Hammer laid out his discovery once again.

"You all might recall the rider I mentioned that come to Burns looking for supplies. Well, I seen him on that same dun. No man is going to forget that beauty or the pissant that was in the saddle."

The lively discussion had gone on awhile when Roy Johnson appeared at the door. His typical cheeriness was absent. "I swear I ain't never seen a horse that big run like Grey. No sir. I couldn't believe these old eyes. Boys, he left 'em in the dust and won going away!"

The marshal jumped from his chair, clapping his hands. Then he slapped Ty on his shoulders. "Hot damn! I knew he would do it. Weren't no doubt about it."

"How come you ain't all smiles, Roy? Grey's alright, I hope."

"Oh, he's fine, Marshal. Problem is, we is fixing to lose them hard-earned dollars we all done bet, 'cause Juan weren't on him at the finish. Come to think of it, Juan wasn't on him much after the start, neither. Don't think anything important got busted up. He spent some time in the air, I swear he did, and he come down hard! He couldn't recall nothing after he come to. Maria went to fetch Doc Diederich when I come this way."

A drawn-out silence followed the news. Finally, the

marshal recovered. "I was sure counting on that money, but I tell you this; we sure got some real good information that Hammer here brung us. Seems like our all-in is looking more promising. It damn sure does."

Later, a soft rain had begun to fall as the last of the race-goers were departing and rounding up their scattered children. The majority of them streamed past the house as the men talked on excitedly. Ben McCullough had joined them, confirming that Roy's description of the Hogan horses matched the four that spent a considerable time around Ty's corral. Eventually, those riders had departed near the north boundary of the ranch. Many other people had stopped to admire the horses inside the corral, but the four Hogan-horse riders seemed to be especially fascinated by the entire layout.

Sitting alone as the evening set in, Ty felt a familiar instinct beginning to surface. It brought him back to his years with Ben and the danger that often came with the territory. Earlier word had come that Juan would be laid up for a day or two, but only his pride was truly damaged. The final piece of surprising news came from the marshal; it was passed onto Ben when he had gone to town for the mail. A woman had reported her brother-in-law had his throat slashed by a big Indian. It was in the dead of night. It seemed he had appeared out of the grass. The brother-in-law had been drunk and intending to rape her when suddenly, he was lifted off his feet from behind, then his neck was cut open.

After the killing, the Indian carried her back to her house, then disappeared. The pitch-black night had made it hard to describe much about him. It was clear the woman had no remorse for her dead in-law. She had described him as a vicious man who could have easily killed her in the state he was in. "Good riddance" was how she had described his death. The fact it was the same night the horses were stolen near her little, sad house left no doubt the big Indian was a member of the night-prowling raiders. These horse thieves would not stop short of killing; the ranchers would most likely have gotten wind of it, shortening the burning fuse.

At first light, the marshal would be making his way to the scene of the raid and throat slashing. Of greater promise, it seemed the raiders had nibbled at the bait; but would they take it hook, line, and sinker? In due time, Ty's thoughts were broken by the presence of Liz and little Ty. Liz looked as fetching as ever as she handed little DT to his open arms. "There is some new wine. Why don't we find out if it suits us?" she offered proudly.

"We need you to pay us some attention, DT, don't we?" Ty tossed DT up from his chest, then softly caught him. DT held his stubby arms up, begging for another toss. Ty obliged, setting off a round of gleeful giggling. Liz handed him a cup of deep purple wine and seated herself beside him and the squirming boy.

"Ty, I am becoming very uneasy. I find myself mad at this whole situation, with you in the middle of it all. When that many strangers came around the place, I got frightened. Especially when I saw Ben's face change when he discovered the four riders lingering near the corral. He couldn't take his eyes off them or their horses. Somehow, he sensed these men were dangerous visitors."

Ty sipped from his cup. "This is real fine, Liz. You done good. I knew you would, 'cause you always do."

"Don't you dare change the subject, Ty McCord, or I am going to rip that mane of yours right off your hard head!"

Ty smiled over the top of his cup, taking joy in Liz's fiery manner. "Ben truly loved Millie Hogan, Liz. They was as close as can be. Ain't no doubt in my mind, Liz, if he was certain any of them gawkers killed Millie, he might just have shot him right there."

"I don't doubt it, Ty," she agreed, running her hands

through her ample auburn hair. "Your ranger days were over, then you go and get yourself all tangled up in this mess."

"I gave the marshal my word, Liz. You know that."

The fear in her eyes conflicted him between regret and his instinct to conclude the puzzling raids that threatened the tallgrass ranchers. He wanted to hold her, but he knew she would have none of it. Also, he knew something in his nature would not allow him to hug her or admit his own fear for her, DT, and the life he craved.

Sim's Time

The races had concluded two days ago, but the men seemed to never stop chirping about them. In the dead times of the last few months, the crude shelters had acquired rough doors attached with heavy leather hinges. Deadfall from nearby trees had been gathered and stacked around the base of the shelters to keep out little varmints and snakes. Deer and other skins were drying here and there in the constant winds.

"Sim, it's a damn shame you weren't at them races," Jake was saying.

"Jake ain't wrong, neither, boss," Dusty piped in. "Me and Zeb and Peak done a good bit of eyeballin' round them spreads. One I seen before awhile back, told you about it, too. Right near the races, so we looked it over nice-like. Took our time checkin' things. Our friend Mr. Clifford would pay top dollar for what's penned there in that big corral. That's not all, neither. I reckon we seen over two thousand head of longhorns if we seen *one*! It ain't all fenced in, but what is is tended to by good hands.

It was early evening. The orange sky was vaguely visible and sliding away behind the rolling hills in the west. Sim rolled a smoke up. Two small fire pits were burning new, dry wood gathered for the evening meal. With the exception of Breed, his men seemed ready for a new raid. Since the next delivery would quite likely be the last, some had begun to discuss their individual plans. Some talked of staying on as hands on Sim's spread of the future, wherever it was going to be located in the tallgrass. The uncommonly cool evening, along with the good humor of his men, seemed to be right for passing out some recently acquired whiskey.

Zeb did the honors for Sim. The whiskey was gratefully accepted. Sim carefully approached Breed, who seemed to be mumbling to himself. Sim sat on the ground beside him, saying nothing for a time. Breed did not look toward him, only at the small signs he had drawn in the dirt. Among the riders, Breed was the single man that struck unwanted fear in him. A careful approach was always warranted. Breed remained silent.

"Why did you kill him, Breed? We ain't had no problems. Now there will be questions."

"He deserved to die," Breed whispered.

"No. You could have silenced him and not killed him."

"A blue coat raped my mother before my eyes. I don't forget. This man had a gun. He deserved to die. Only weak men do such things."

"I ain't happy, Breed."

"Don't matter none. Man's dead," Breed said grimly.

Sim, aware the conversation had ended, made his way toward Zeb and the whiskey jug. Peak, Zeb, and Dusty Nelson were leaning casually against a long hitching rail. Peak was leading the conversation. When Sim approached, Zeb handed him the bottle.

"Why we all penned up, Sim? We done all seen them fine horses waiting for the taking," Peak said confrontationally. "Them horses is worth a heap of money."

Sim ignored the comment. He had vowed long ago to disregard any suggestions from the young hothead. In the distance, loud thunder rolled through the prairie. Soon strong, cool winds began to whip through the trees and thickets. Miles of grass gave way to the will of it. Worries forced on him by men such as Breed and Peak would soon just be memories. When he took his rightful place in the vast prairie, he'd wipe them from his mind.

The last gathering of ranch horses would not be rushed. It would be the most carefully planned of all. He was of a mind to consider all things that could threaten success, such as Breed's need for vengeance. He would bide his time, hurried by no man.

Chapter 29

Grandfather Winds

Three quiet and uneventful weeks passed following the excitement of the races—almost long enough for Juan to recover from the humiliation of the race. A prideful man, his recovery was slower than most men. Roy had taken charge of driving nearly five hundred head of cattle to Abilene. Juan and the other top hands, along with a few neighbor boys, accomplished it in less than a week. Not a longhorn was lost.

The dog days of the prairie summer arrived with blistering heat as well as constant winds. Ty entered the open door of the marshal's office and sat down in a worn, old, straight-backed chair.

"It's gonna be one of them days, Ty. Hotter than a fresh forest fire. Coffee?"

"Reckon I will," Ty said gratefully.

"I been all over these parts, Ty. I ain't seen a big Indian of any kind. No one else has, either. Used to be a man would see them Kaws in these parts. That Dixon woman don't seem like one that would conjure up no tall tale," the marshal revealed grimly. "I was plumb encouraged directly after that race business. Them raiders is laying low. Now the whole damn situation is eatin' my innards. Even the wife says she don't like being around me these days. Says I ain't no good to nobody. She ain't wrong. I must admit."

"We're sitting on a powder keg. No two ways about it," Ty added, sitting his empty cup on the marshal's desk. "I sure ain't been no help," Ty said honestly, "but I am convinced the raiders ain't gone. They got no reason whatsoever to vanish. These ranches 'round here being so far apart had to have whet their appetite more than a little bit. Seeing them up close in the daylight for one long day is what's going to drive them bastards out the hole they crawled in."

"And if you're wrong?" the marshal demanded.

"Well, I see it this way: I am fixing to be fired, and you will have to find another damn lawman."

"That ain't near being funny, Ty."

"It wasn't intended to be, I reckon," Ty lied. "I've always heard these plains Indians believe all life evolves from the wind. 'Grandfather Wind' is how they speak of it. Comes from the sea. Creates the hunted and the hunter. I say we wait it out. Wait for Grandfather Wind to deliver the hunted to the hunters."

"Come to think of it, Ty, wind is something folks around here can damn sure depend on. This here situation is eating me up inside. I ain't sleepin' none, neither. A big old burr oak got struck by lightning a ways ago at my place. So I set about cuttin' it down last week. I done worked on it at night when I can't sleep. Must be three years of firewood I been splittin'."

Ty felt sorry for the sulking marshal. The man was truly working himself into a sinkhole of frustration. He would talk to Doc Diederich the next time they crossed paths. Ty wasn't given to talking about his own thoughts along the same lines, but the simple fact was, he had not been a help to the marshal whatsoever. The races had showed some promise, but it was slipping away. Could it be the Hogan-horse riders had simply left the grass? If they had, then why, when not a single person had threatened the night raids? Hope was flapping in the hot winds.

At suppertime, even old Ben McCullough had put in his thoughts, saying he would of swore he had smelled the thieves at the races, but he, too, was just grabbing at straws. The old lawman and soldier simply wanted revenge for Millie's death. Even at his advanced age, Ty knew he would not hesitate to shoot to kill if given half a chance. Losing Millie had been a devastating loss to him. Since his arrival, Liz had taken charge of his grief; she either kept him busy or kept him chatting. He had taken to DT as a grandfather might, and DT buzzed around him constantly. It was clear Ben would not be on the trail back to Guyman anytime soon.

"I swear to God, Liz, that gooseberry pie is every bit as good as Millie's," he said over his empty plate. Liz smiled and kissed him on his wind-burned forehead. Ty loved her for her tender way with Ben.

Although he was not a man familiar with depending on others, Liz had simply worked her determined way into his deep-seated self-reliance, making him depend on her whether he was comfortable about it or not. Now Ben, too, had fallen for her womanly strength. Ty and Ben both needed her in different ways.

The next day, following his visit with the marshal, Ty made a deposit with banker Wendling, who was more than pleased with the results of the cattle Ty had delivered to Abilene. "It ain't going to be long before I reckon you will be the biggest spread around here. Say, I hear they's plans being made for next summer's race. People in town can't stop jawin' about it. Too bad about that big stallion of yours throwing that little Mex halfway to Medicine Lodge," he said humorously.

After departing the bank, Ty stopped into the general store for sugar, salt, and more cheroots. It was a boiling-hot day that seemed to have sent even the ever-present birds for shelter. The town dogs were nowhere to be seen, having sought shade or shelter out of the energy-draining sun. Nothing seemed to be moving. Everyone and everything was driven from their normal routine. Mounting Grey, Ty noticed the familiar buggy of the area's traveling man of the cloth rolling into the street. Ty halted Grey. The preacher, dressed in a black suit and tie, waved his hello. "I am on a mission, friend," he declared as the streams of sweat gathered the dust on his face before falling on his drenched shirt.

"How's that?" Ty asked, lighting a fresh smoke.

"With the hand of the God, my mission is to save sinners from the fires of hell."

Ty adjusted his Stetson for more shade. "From the feel of things, seems like they already arrived."

"Oh, brother. It's never too late to be washed of your sins," the wild-eyed preacher announced.

Ty touched the brim of his hat, slow-trotting away from the jabbering man. The oppressive heat lingered on until the month's end. Still no signs of the raiders had surfaced—nor had an Indian of any description.

Skylined

"Elvira come apart at the seams and threw me plumb out of our house," the marshal revealed, as the men sipped Liz's lemonade. "I was splitting them burr oak logs half the night!" Liz smiled widely while she refilled Austin's glass.

"Ty might be joining you soon, Marshal," she said, as she retreated from her porch.

"Neighbor woman come by the jail this morning, mad as a wet hen. Seems she got wind of the rancher group fixin' to pay some hired guns to find them thieves," the marshal said dejectedly. "I reckon I could try to talk to them boys one last time, but they ain't gonna pay me no mind."

"Who's running the show with them ranchers?" Ben McCullough asked.

"Two hardnosed men that been in the grass a mite longer than me. Names're Shag Bellemere and Luke Mehrer. They's stirrin' the pot."

"Liz speaks highly of the wives," Ty interjected glumly. "I met 'em at a horse sale awhile back. Both was the type that could drive a real hard bargain. Right friendly, though."

The conversation continued well into the night, with the marshal sleeping in the tack room Hammer had occupied almost two months previously. At first light, Ben appeared with a steaming cup of coffee for the marshal. Ben felt sorry for him. The man was in a real fix with nowhere to turn. He was downright weary and not thinking clearly. In some ways, Ben could relate to his sad situation.

"Doc Diederich wants to take a look-see about my lumbago. Why don't I ride into town with you? We could get some grub at the hotel."

"Much obliged, Ben. Don't feel right staying 'round here and putting Liz out. Besides, she made it real clear it's *my* fault Ty's all roped up in this nightmare."

"Ty says he's got a mind to erect a new ranch house and plans to use the limestone around here. Liz says she and DT is going to Kansas City soon to look for house things in them fancy stores. Probably be gone a week or more."

"Well, one less person nippin' at my behind would be good. No doubt about that."

Ben returned to the ranch late in the afternoon. A cool, welcome breeze accompanied him. He found Roy, Juan, and Ty at the corral. Juan was waving his arms and pointing in the direction of the fading sunlight.

"Me and Roy was working the west pasture just below them sharp, sloping hills, when we seen two riders skylined on top of the one to the north. A heifer was hung up down in that muddy slew, so we was in the trees and water. That heifer up and kicked Roy in the leg real hard. It sent Roy to dancing. When he looked up, there they was. Then he came and got me. I seen 'em, too, perched up there. Meester McCord, they bided their time before moving on."

"I got my work done, so I done come to visit Juan. Then that big heifer got all stuck in the mud. She put a knot on my leg the size of a cow pie," Roy said regretfully.

Ty leaned his back against the rails. The others waited for his reaction. "Well, our neighbors seen this place many a time. Liz has always welcomed anyone. Whoever they was, looks like they was comfortable enough not to fret about being skylined." The notion the two riders were part of the missing raiders gang was stuck between his brain and lips.

"I say we keep a couple of us in the pastures, out of sight, for the next few days."

"Marshal Seward ain't got nowhere to go these days. Nobody's in the hoosegow, neither. Me and the marshal will take the next two nights," Ben volunteered happily. "I'll bring my glasses. They might help some if there is another visit. Those limestone bluffs is right near that dead-end trail just a little east of those steep hills. Staying unnoticed won't be no problem at all."

Ty could see Ben welcomed his idea. "Three hundred head of horns in that pasture, too. Most has been hiding from the blasted heat in the hollows. I'll give them a good look-over, Ty," Ben said excitedly. "Finding the marshal is best left up to me."

A gentle breeze was caressing the leaves of the cotton-woods when Ben settled in under a limestone outcropping the following day. Some scattered clouds arrived with the waning hours of the afternoon. A number of lean long-horns lingered in the shade nearby, shivering and swatting away ever-present insects with their tails. Nearly a mile away, Marshal Seward sat enjoying his pipe. Concealed next to an overhang, he was allowed an unobstructed view of the two steep-sloped hilltops. He was a sad, troubled man. Owls hooted away, and little birds flitted in and out of the trees and the straight-stemmed prairie plants. It seemed his proud existence was going to hell in a handbasket. Grass-hidden bobwhites carried on, while a half dozen black turkey vultures rode the wind in their effortless circles above, as if waiting to feast on his rotting carcass.

The next morning, Ben found him sleeping soundly beneath a thick cedar. Sensing an intruder, the marshal jumped awkwardly to his feet.

"Sorry, Ben," he said pridefully. "I faded just before sunup. Guess them horns sung me to sleep. I was fine in them night hours. Ain't used to sleeping much these days, no how. What there was of it helped a bit."

Ben climbed onto his saddled little filly. He waited patiently while the marshal cinched up his saddle and mounted.

"Liz's hotcakes is waitin' for us by now."

"They's something to look forward towards, Ben. Ain't been much else, though. If'n I didn't have you to talk to these days, I don't know what I'd do. Elvira ain't showin' no signs of comin' down from her high horse. She's refusing to admit I'm even alive. The McCords is workin' sunup to sundown, and them other boys is busy workin' cattle and enjoyin' their ladies. Jesus, it's a rare thing to have anybody in town even speak to me. A man could say I done been put out to pasture."

"You're having a devil of a time; no doubt about that, Marshal. But I got me a strong feeling them night-roamin' thieves is nibbling on fine horse bait."

Propping up the downtrodden marshal had become a full time job for Ben. Stretching the truth was just plain necessary at times like these. They rode in silence until they arrived at the ranch. Liz waved them into their waiting breakfast, where Ty sat with his coffee.

"Them Texas 'horns is beginning to fill out just fine, Ty," Ben said.

"We both seen most of them down that way, because they was bunched in them hollows," the marshal said wearily. "All we seen otherwise was varmints and birds."

"Marshal, you look like you ain't had no shut-eye in a month," Ty said seriously.

"I'm a mite shy of it," he admitted sadly.

"I got some horse work for today, but I plan on filling in tonight. Liz is making demands for you staying here so you can do some catching up. Log splittin' is not tolerated, neither. Just make yourself at home in the tack room. There is blackberry wine in the storm cellar. It might help you a bit. Going against Liz's wishes is not recommended 'round here. Bein' marshal don't carry no more weight than me."

"I reckon I'm fightin' enough losing battles as it is. I don't need no more."

"Now don't you dare take sick on us, Marshal. That's good wine; drink all you care to. It's the best I've made. It will set you to sleeping after a bit," Liz said.

The following night of hill gazing proved just as fruitless for Ben and Ty. Morning came on by bringing with it black, voluminous, threatening clouds. A light rain began to bless the grasses and the dry, ancient buffalo wallows began to fill up with water. Ben and Ty forded a little, shallow creek. The horses clattered on its limestone, and they exited the water up a wet, rock-strewn bank, sending a handful of strutting turkeys to short flight. They rode on through the cottonwoods with grim determination.

The rain continued to fall throughout the day, and, much to the delight of Liz, Marshal Seward had yet to show himself.

Chapter 31

Lightning Strikes

Roy and Juan arrived, set to go.

"We seen about everything but the riders in them hills last night," Ben offered dejectedly. They filled their canteens, and Liz provided them with biscuits and coffee. Departing, Juan followed Roy as they trotted toward the hills in the steady rain. Loud sky-violence cracked and boomed somewhere in the distant southern vastness. Tall cottonwoods and oaks bent to the will of the building winds.

Roy told Juan about the Gulf of Mexico he had seen in his youth, saying the tallgrass reminded him of the rolling waves. Roy chose a high, rocky perch affording a wide view of the surroundings, including the McCord ranch house, vaguely visible in the rain. A convenient indentation provided some protection from the rain. His horse was picketed far below, amid some thick pines. Juan seemed determined to seek much higher ground somewhere near the southern reach of the ever-expanding ranch. The two had been acquaintances in Dodge, but since arriving in the tallgrass, the strongest of friendships had developed between them. Juan's tireless manner and constant chatter concealed a certain grittiness Roy couldn't help but notice. Juan's days as a deputy in Oklahoma seemed still embedded in him.

As the ink-black darkness of the night enveloped the hills, Roy felt positive that his agile little friend would not fall victim to the desire for sleep. The brewing storm seemed headed in their direction. Sleep for anyone would come grudgingly, at best. Several massive, white bolts of lightning tore through the blackness, illuminating the heaving grass and the hills as if mid-day had suddenly come; rain cascaded down from his perch like it was a waterfall—this was not good for a man who was counting on no obstructions to his view.

Soon, another deafening drumroll of thunder brought with it reverberations and withering blasts of lightning. High-noon brightness came and lingered. For an instant, Roy saw clearly a tall, sitting rider at the widest expanse of the pasture. Then, in a second, the black night reappeared. They had come back!

Dawn came on with a partial clearing of skies. Below and not far away, Juan rode slowly toward his wet perch; he had the appearance of a drowned rat. Scrambling down the slick hillside, Roy saddled his horse and waited.

"Ain't seen a storm like that one in don't know how many years," he said, when Juan pulled up next to him.

"Roy, I was plenty afraid," Juan admitted. "I seen another rider, though. Clear as day," he said.

"I seen him too, Juan. Way over yonder along the fence line." Roy pointed toward the east boundary. "Stood out like a sore thumb when that giant bolt plunged itself down. I come close to going deaf under that overhang too, right before he got hisself all lit up. Every living thing scattered and run for cover, 'cept him."

"A no-good man, I am sure. Things is tallying up bad for Meester McCord," Juan added, as they trotted off. Searching for the intruder's tracks wasn't a possibility following such a storm.

More threatening storm clouds arrived with the dark of the following evening. Damp, heavy winds greeted Ben and Ty as they rode into the hills once again. Distant rumblings promised yet another unsettled, storm-laced night.

"It don't seem to want to let up none, Ty," Ben remarked. "We may not be able to see at all. It's blacker than Liz's coffee out here, and it seems to be gettin' worse. You reckon we shoulda took her advice and stayed put?"

"More than likely," Ty said gloomily, as big drops of new rain began to pop on the rim of his hat. "I'm plumb sick of coming up empty-handed in this here affair," Ty said with noticeable frustration. "Since we can't depend on seein' anything at the moment, why don't we get ourselves under that big undercut where them flat rocks jut out some. Over yonder, where the creek makes a big bend," he further clarified. "We'll be dry there."

"That's good," Ben said seriously. "I want to discuss a recent decision I done locked onto. I ain't getting' no younger, Ty. It's important to me."

Lightning cracked not far away. The undercut was just big enough for them to avoid the rain. Below, the creek roared, and barely visible gray vapors hung over the rushing water.

"Ty, here's what I done. I sent a wire to a lawyer friend of mine in Guyman, telling him to put my little place, along with the stables, up for sale. If something should go bad with me before things is wrapped up, he was instructed to make you and Liz rightful owners. What's more, I'm fixin' to stay put right here in the tallgrass. I ain't been this happy since Millie has been gone. Liz and DT is like family to me now. You are the son I never had. I figured you already knew that part."

"I don't rightly know what to say, Ben."

"You don't have to say nothing. That's just the way things are gonna shake out with my affairs."

"I don't suppose you done planned this all out so's you could keep on eatin' Liz's cooking," Ty asked happily.

"That's as fine a reason as any, I reckon," Ben answered.

Rain began to fall in sheets as more lightning and thunder worked their loud ways toward them, invading the mineshaft blackness of the night. It was well after midnight when the rain and noise finally stopped. Sudden stillness came with heavy air. Saddled up and moving, the two lawmen set about looking for more riders they would not find.

"This here air feels like a wet horse blanket on my shoulders. Not only that, them bitin' little devils is coming in swarms. It seems like I'm special to 'em. Tornadoes come alive in nights like this. I reckon we both seen plenty of them in our day to last a lifetime."

"They're nasty, alright," Ty added.

Eventually, they came to the last hill bordering the south end of the ranch, a naked hill by most standards. Grey and Ben's horse clicked and tapped their shoes on the flat rock, snorting a zigzag path to the top, where a few lonely trees stood like sentries.

In the west reaches of the prairie and what had been obstructed by the hill was a bright, constant white-and-yellow glow in the night sky.

"Fire," Ty yelled.

Carefully they descended the tall hill. "Ben, go on to the ranch. Let the marshal know. I'll head towards that fire. The river is too high for crossin' here. I'll have to go around it for awhile. You best stay with Liz and DT."

Once on a narrow road, Ty let Grey have his way.

Diversion

Chapter 32

"You got yerself a problem, Peak?" Sim asked bitterly.

"You're damn right I do. I don't fancy none of this sweat-lodge heat. Let's get this shindig movin'. We been sittin' here long enough. Ain't possible to get no darker out here, anyways."

"Why don't you quit your yappin', Peak," Jake said angrily.

The anxious riders were well concealed in the midst of a thick stand of trees and orange hedge fronted by three grass-covered mounds the size of a buffalo. The fire was now out of control. A rising number of men and women continued to arrive, but it was far too late to salvage any part of the schoolhouse.

"I figure Breed should be close enough," Zeb Hernandez said quietly. "Most of the men folks around here has done shown up or is likely on the way.

Minutes later, Sim led his men through a narrow opening in the trees behind them. Torching the school would surely have drawn the attention of all but a few of the surrounding inhabitants.

Juan was the first to see Ty arrive. "Maria seen the flames before me, Meester McCord. We couldn't sleep none—too much noise and terrible heat. Funny thing, though. We seen no lightning near the school, Meester McCord. Our leetel house is just a short distance away, toward town. Me and Maria, we would have seen it, as certain as Mary is the Blessed Mother. But look at this!"

In his hand was a charred, broken axe handle that had the half-burned remains of several rags wired to it.

"This school was torched! Perhaps this one bounced off the school. The others, well, they went through the windows, 'cause I seen they all was shattered. The fire was blazing inside. We could do nothing to stop it. After awhile, Roy came along with some hands from a nearby ranch. Help was all too late, 'cept being sure the fire weren't gonna spread none," Juan continued dejectedly. "Maria, she went back to the Diamond D with Sonia Mae. Why destroy a little schoolhouse, Ty?"

"It comes to mind it just might draw the folks around here's attention while something else is taking place. Stealin' horses seems a strong possibility. You and Roy, hightail it back to my place. It's best you both come armed!"

Ty reasoned that if it *was* his remuda the night riders wanted, they would be in no hurry, so as not to draw unwanted attention by happenstance. Confidence would be with them as long as the school burned brightly. In the worst of nights, why else would strangers appear around his ranch? It all made sense to his racing mind. Grey thundered down the road once again, leaving the flaming school behind.

Liz and DT would be fast asleep, but Ben would rise to the bark of the dog, regardless of what disturbed her. Old Danny didn't tolerate strangers, no matter the time of day. Certain danger gripped Ty's senses as Grey raced toward the ranch, images of DT and Liz vivid in his racing mind. Strangers in the black, stormy night must have a plan; most likely, the burning schoolhouse was part of it. All of the last year's raids in the tallgrass were accomplished in darkness, aided by extreme weather at times. It all seemed to fit.

Like nothing else, raging fire drew townsfolk and ranchers to it like flies to raw meat. It rendered precious horses and cattle vulnerable. Only Ben stood between Ty's remuda and a pack of thieves—if that *was* their destination. Deep inside Ty was an unwavering conviction that the night raiders had taken the bait and were headed in the direction of his prized possessions.

Finally departing the muddy road, he sought the safety of the trees and thickets. He stopped long enough to retrieve his peacemaker and holster from his saddlebag. He strapped it on and tied it down on his leg, while Grey drank greedily from a little puddle. Slipping into the saddle once again, they moved cautiously toward the silhouette of the ranch house. Nothing on him was dry. Sodden spider webs from the trees hung on his hat. Limp tree limbs raked him and tore at his clothes. His breathing was a slow discipline. Alert and calm of mind, he moved on swiftly, ignoring all but his destination. Listening for uncommon night sounds, he slowed Grey's pace, then he slid quietly from the saddle and patted his powerful drenched companion. Insects feasted on them as they drew near a low rise that afforded Ty a clear view of his corral. Then, without warning, a silent figure struck Ty viciously from behind, slamming his face down into the grass. There, he lost consciousness from the blow.

A dark, tall figure grasped Grey's limp reins and leaped into the saddle. In an instant, Grey reared on his haunches, pitching the robed intruder skyward like a rag doll. The man landed awkwardly, his head crashing on a large, jagged rock. He lay still, with unblinking eyes staring skyward into the vast blackness. Grey shivered and snorted, pawing the dirt and grass nearby.

Some distance away, the riders waited nervously.

"Damn it to hell, Sim. Where is Breed? We should

have seen him in the corral by now," Peak said angrily. "We been sitting in these here trees long enough. What you waiting for anyhow? No tellin' what Breed decided to do."

"Shut up, Peak," Dusty Nelson said angrily. You ain't running this outfit."

"Breed never failed us before, Peak," Zeb added. "What's bothering you anyhow? You losing your nerve?"

Sim kept his own worry to himself. Something didn't seem right, though. Maybe this final raid riled him. The men were jittery as all hell. Without a sighting of Breed, he had to make a decision. Before they had departed, he had made certain Breed understood another killing would not be tolerated.

"We wait. I'll tell you when," he said forcefully, while hiding his own growing suspicions. "Jake, start picking your way toward the corral; if'n Breed don't show, go about openin' that back gate and get them horses movin'. We'll run 'em through that far south holler, then cross the creek."

Dogged

When finally Ty came to, terrible pain ravaged his swollen head. How long he had laid in the grass, he didn't know. Feeling the gash on his skull, he tried to clear his vision and rise to his feet. A short distance from him lay the unmoving form of a man. His head was at an odd angle. Insects were invading his mouth and nostrils. Death had come unexpectedly, no doubt, for this Indian that Juan and Roy had seen before. Ty tried to focus his eyes in the darkness, to no avail. It seemed a hundred locusts were cranking away inside his head, as if to drive him insane. Blood-streaked sweat ran down his neck. He slapped his face hard in an attempt to clear his buzzing head. The night riders had to be close, but where? Instantly, he felt for his Colt. Unrelenting blackness and heavy heat held onto the night. Grey stepped close to him, shivering and swatting with his tail. Ty leaned his tall frame against the beast, feeling for his Winchester in the saddle scabbard.

"He damn well had it coming, boy," Ty murmured, while glancing at the dead intruder.

Grudgingly, his hearing began to return with sounds of soft-lowing longhorns and distant coyote howls. A half mile away, ten quiet horsemen deserted the safety of the trees. Saddle-high grass gave them the appearance of half-men floating above its tallness. Conversation had given way to alertness. Only an occasional horseshoe on pasture rock or flushing birds made their presence known. Sim led his men carefully. His nerves were on edge without the presence of Breed. Had Breed used his knife again, Sim wondered?

With the exception of Jake, Zeb's eyesight was the best of all his men. He would signal the presence of Jake inside the corral, or perhaps Breed. This was the blackest of nights that Sim could recall. A few more minutes expired before the corral became visible.

Up ahead, Jake felt confident he was undetected, as he slip-knotted his black gelding behind the barn, preventing anyone noticing him from the ranch house. Only one light shone through the windows in the rear of the house. Two cats with glowing eyes watched when he stepped between the rails into the corral.

Sim raised his arm high enough for all the riders to see. They stopped. Zeb rode on. Soon enough the riders heard his birdlike whistle signal. A man was in the confines of the sturdy corral! It was little Jake.

Jake's mind remained cluttered with his thoughts of the missing "Silent One" as he opened the gate and stepped among the fidgeting, shifting prize remuda. Bats dipped and dived all around in frenzied pursuit of the night's insects. Sim's riders positioned themselves soundlessly as the first of the horses ran through the open corral.

Unexpectedly, a low, guttural growl came from outside of the rails. Commencing to bark loudly, the dog sprang at Jake and sank teeth into his knee, holding on tenaciously. Reaching for his pistol, Jake whipped it across the dog's snout—to no avail. Suddenly, something hot tore into his shoulder, knocking him backward into the mud. There was a man with a rifle standing in the doorway behind the ranch house. Another shot rang out, sending the man in the doorway down hard.

"Git, Jake!" Sim yelled desperately, as the last of the

remuda raced into the night, surrounded by his riders. In an instant, Dusty was at Jake's side, kicking the dog violently as he shouldered his bleeding friend. Throwing the bleeding rider on his horse, Dusty fetched his gelding and raced away.

Alerted by the commotion, Ty had mounted Grey. He could now clearly see his remuda disappearing southward. He had a hard decision to make. As rapidly as he could, Ty raced to the house.

Liz met him at the door, gripped with fear. "You been hurt!" she cried when she saw him. "Ben's been shot, too. Roy and Juan just arrived. Roy's now on his way to fetch Doc Diederich."

"You okay, Liz? What about DT?"

"I'm fine. DT slept through the whole thing. Your head is godawful gashed, Ty!"

"Don't worry none 'bout me. Where's Juan?"

"He ran down to the corral to check on Danny. He said something about the schoolhouse burning down."

"I'll need to take a few more cartridges with me." Ty grabbed two boxes off a shelf. "Juan and me will be leaving directly. Them riders got a good lead."

"Don't you dare, Ty! Let them be, they'll not return. There is no reason now. Ben's in his room and in grave condition," Liz admitted tearfully. "Roy and Juan got him settled as best they could."

"I put one of them thieving bastards on his back, Ty," Ben said in a hesitating, shallow voice, when Ty entered his room. Ben looked to be in dire shape. "Find 'em Ty," he whispered with determination. Ty held the old man's hand for a brief moment then gave Ben a confirming nod.

Juan bounced into the house just as Ty prepared to leave. "Old Danny is a tough one, Meester McCord. She don't seem to have nothing broke up. Took a beating, she did. Got one ugly cut on her snout."

Ty turned to face Liz. "The marshal and Doc Died-

erich will be here directly. Tell them me and Juan are goin'
out the south gate, and there's a dead Indian in the trees
along the east fence line. Shouldn't be no fuss pickin' up
our trail. Roy will ride with him, so with two sets of good
eyes, they're bound to find us. Might as well simmer down
a bit. Ben and DT need you now. I am of a mind for no
conversation."

Swiftly, Ty and Juan galloped into the waning blackness and disappeared. "Maria, she makes good jerky. I
got plenty," Juan announced. "Real fine. I brung a sack of
cornbread. Last us a day or so I reckon. There's coffee in
my canteen, too."

Crossing a rushing stream, they clambered up a steep
embankment. They stopped only long enough for Ty to
drop a bright silver rifle cartridge in a bare rocky spot on
the worn trail. Soon a new dawn came on brightly. The
raiders' muddy tracks soon gave way to the drenched tallgrass. Ty dropped another cartridge at the point where the
night riders exited the worn trail and entered the grass.
"Don't look like they slowed down none for the man Ben
plugged," Ty said. "They ain't about to stop for nobody."

Horse-crushed, waist-high grass soon led them once
again back to the same little creek flowing swiftly out of
its banks. The escape was well thought out. "They'll be
stickin' to the water where they can, I reckon, Juan. Then
I imagine they will try a switchback somewhere. I'd do that
if I was in their boots." Another cartridge was dropped in
the sand, where it would be easily noticed. Juan took the
lead entering the water.

The bright morning sun's rays glistened through the
wet, overhanging tree limbs. As they progressed, Ty's
thoughts drifted back to Ben, Liz, and little DT. The
ranch had continued to grow, along with DT. Ty dreamed
of the future with Liz in her new home. She would have
it as she wanted. If Ben survived, they would be near to
watch over him. He could live out his days grandfathering

DT and watching Ty's growing herd. Nothing short of an act of God was going to disturb that.

Without any question, there would be a price to pay when this wild goose chase was concluded. Often, words had eluded him at the worst moments. Ignoring Liz and speaking gruffly was wrong. She had been afraid for Ben and DT and the life they had built for themselves. His ways nagged at him. She needed more, and yet he had pulled up short once again. She deserved to extract her piece of his stubborn hide. Hurting his fiery wife was wrong. He would have to do better somehow.

"Meester McCord, look here!" Juan yelled, while pointing at some tracks on a little rocky upslope near the creek. "They come out here." Ty drew up next to him. Clear tracks were scattered on the bank. Ty could see the lure of the chase in Juan's eyes. It had its grip on him now. Leaving a cartridge there, they moved slowly up a stumpy hill, past a burned-out log hut. Some turkey feathers scattered by the morning breeze, the remains of a losing struggle with an efficient predator.

Often, they followed the tracks on foot. Ty recalled his old friend, Tall Fox, a tracker who would notice signs Ty couldn't recognize or see himself. "Juan, I speak the truth. That crafty old Cheyenne had himself a downright amazing ability. An hombre had himself a pack of real trouble if Tall Fox was on his trail. We'd be a sight better off right now if he was ridin' with us. He seen more from the back of his horse than I could down all fours. That's no lie," he declared honestly.

High noon brought with it the promise of another energy sapping, hot afternoon. The two soon stopped in a stand of lanky cottonwoods. Dismounting, they sought the contents of their saddlebags before they settled under the trees while the horses lapped from the stream behind them.

Juan looked up from the cornbread and jerky in his

hands. Persistent winds rustled through the trees as he spoke. "These riders, they cross that stream four times. It had to make for slow going, bein' they might have trouble with all them horses of yours, Meester McCord."

"True enough, I suppose, and don't forget they have a wounded man, too. Well, that is one way of lookin' at the situation, Juan, but we been slowed down to a snail's pace. They ain't no fools, neither. I reckon they might split up at some point. To my way of thinkin', they mighta done it by now. One of them boys is shot up real bad, according to Ben. Unless he's dead now, he ain't likely to be left nowheres. I've seen a time or two when a man's compadres helped out with the dyin' part though. Especially when their hides was in jeopardy."

Shortly, the spring-fed little creek that had refreshed them was forded once again by the determined trackers. Steady heat and wind accompanied them, until finally, the fading light signaled the end of their day. On a lightning-ravaged hill where they camped, some freshly downed trees provided shelter for the night.

"Maybe Roy and the marshal seen them cartridges," Ty said while starting the fire. "I reckon if they're coming to find us, this fire up here might be a help."

Chapter 34

Cartridge Trail

Back in the hidden corral, Dusty stared down at Jake lying in a rough bunk. "He needs a doctor, Sim, or else he's done."

"I ain't blind, Dusty, but we don't have no time for no sawbones," Sim said abruptly. "He is going to Abilene with us tomorrow. We can find a doctor there." A cold, evil expression was etched on Sim's face.

"That's a death sentence, boss!" Sim turned his back to Dusty and walked away.

Jake was covered in blood, and his breathing was uneven, his eyes half closed. Dusty cleaned the wounds as best he could, then he put a wet rag to Jake's bloodless face. Words deserted Dusty as he watched his desperate friend struggle to stay conscious. Hate for Sim welled up within him. Presently, Zeb Hernandez and two others came to pay their respects, for they all knew death was close at hand. Unexpectedly, the little rider seemed to will himself to speak. However, there was no sound, just the movement of his parched lips. Dusty leaned close as the others watched the sad scene.

"What's he trying to say, Dusty?" Zeb asked grimly.

"Only thing I can make out is 'Breed.' He's trying to say 'Breed' time and again." For a moment, Jake's eyes locked onto the man standing there beside him. Then he faded and was dead.

Peak was standing outside when the riders emerged. "Sim don't care none. He'd just as soon see us *all* die, soon as them rides is delivered into Abilene."

"If'n I was you, Peak, I'd be real careful-like what words you spit out 'round here. Some folks might just take offense," Zeb growled as he walked away.

Later, as the hot winds of the day began to fade, Sim gathered his men around him. "We all knowed that in another day or such we ain't safe here no more. So we leave with our horses before dark. I figure whoever is on our trail from that there ranch ain't goin' to give up just yet. Being Breed's flown the coop, when we get to Abilene, there's just a bit more money for all of you. Them ranchers might just be comin' south looking for us, too. Looking at them low-hanging clouds that is blowing in, seems like a fifty-fifty chance rain might just be our partner again. This ain't no time to push our luck too far."

Fifteen miles away, Ty and Juan anxiously examined matted tallgrass and a muddy new path where the night riders had split into two different groups. One went more to the east, and the other was veering in a westerly direction. "Just like I figgered," Ty said seriously.

Deep in the grass, Juan was standing with his hands on his hips, staring at the ground. "There is blood on that big, flat rock over there. Maybe this was where they laid down the shot man, Meester McCord," he said anxiously.

"Looks like it," Ty agreed, while lighting a cheroot. "The bleedin' ain't been stopped, neither. I don't buy these thieves would be hiding stolen horses in two places, mainly because they ain't been threatened none. So let's stick to one trail, Juan, 'cause in my mind, both will eventually end at the same place. Besides, a man can't communicate with another if he is too far away and out of sight. Plus, our limited strength is cut in two. If Roy and the marshal is comin' behind us, we need to mark just one trail for them to follow. We follow the blood trail. Seems to me they went back in the water in no time. Otherwise, with the number of my horses they are pushin', following 'em would be simple—no real problem at all."

Juan nodded in agreement as they mounted up. A short time later, the many tracks led them into the rugged creek once again. It was deeper than before; in some places, the water was stirrup level. Whoever was leading this bunch had planned the escape carefully, Ty mused to himself, as they splashed through the rushing waters. Grey led them in and out of the water several more times as the day lingered. Dark, threatening clouds continued to build. Unexpectedly, they failed to locate where the two trails might have joined up.

Juan spoke up, "You think they plan on not coming together this day?"

"They could stay away from each other until dark, I reckon," Ty said. "Seems to me these rascals are already secure wherever they been holding all the rides they stole in these months. I'm of a mind their leader has some training, probably in the war. He's got some evasion skills that he had to learn the hard way. Up to now, they had some fortunate weather to work with, too. Them dark nights and storms was ideal."

The expected rain soon began to fall, in the waning hours of the late afternoon. The sun had disappeared completely, ensuring yet another advantage for the night riders. Track-destroying torrents seemed certain to follow. Juan unrolled his slicker that had been tied behind his saddle. Ty retrieved his from underneath his saddlebags. Juan's upbeat mood began to change.

"You think the cartridges will be lost with the rains, Meester McCord?"

"Well, the hard truth is most of them will plumb disappear."

Juan donned his slicker and stared at the threatening sky as the two continued on

"Another black night is not what a body in our situation would crave. Looks as though the aces is being dealt to those boys that's been doin' the stealin'," Ty said grimly.

There was thunder and a sudden bolt of lightning in the distance. Large raindrops began to come down as they traveled on. There was no more talk for awhile, only the squeak of their saddles and the patter of rain on their hats and slickers. Dutifully, Ty flipped another cartridge into a rocky space, assuming it would not be so easily washed away. As they progressed, the rain only intensified.

Finally, after an extended period, Ty spoke up. "The rain gods are sure presentin' those thieves an opportunity. If I was them, knowing most likely I was bein' followed, I reckon I'd take the chance to deliver them rides. I sure would."

Surprisingly, Juan said nothing. He was focused on a distant plateau that was partially illuminated by a break in the clouds. Oddly, it stood out as if exempted from the falling rain and darkness. Stopping for a moment, he retrieved some field glasses from his saddlebag and put them to his eyes.

"I have good eyes," he said proudly. "I was sure I saw smoke on that hill. Even through the rain, I saw it, Meester McCord. There is a fire near the hill. Must be protected by a rock shelf or something. Maybe even a roof of some kind."

He handed the glasses to Ty. "I'd be much obliged if you stopped calling me mister, Juan." Adjusting the glasses, he discovered the curling smoke in the distance. "You are damn sure right, Juan. We better check it out." With a broad smile, Juan followed Grey and Ty as they hurried toward the hill. "Don't recall any talk at all of ranchers in these parts, Juan. You put us onto something, I'm hopin'."

Some minutes later, they reined in behind the hill. Smoke continued to elevate on the unseen opposite side of the unusually steep, tall uprising. Snubbing the horses, they drew their rifles from their scabbards and proceeded on foot. Hundreds of yards on the far side of the hill was a lively stream with heavy brush and thickets. They made their way carefully to a high spot in the creek. It provided a shallow crossing, and there, the horses' tracks were plentiful. Another fifty yards farther, between oversized limestone rocks, was a sturdy wooden gate of fallen timbers big enough to open for a dozen horses at a time. Opening the gate carefully, they stepped inside the massive natural corral.

"Why this would hold a hundred horses if it held *one*," Juan said excitedly.

The several rough shelters inside yielded nothing. The largest of them had been struck by lightning. It continued to smolder as smoke rose above the hill. They examined the confines of the hideout, finding nothing of interest until Juan motioned with a hand for Ty to join him in back of the smoldering sod-and-timber shelter. A fresh dirt mound lay under a jutting overhang of the hill. It had been carefully covered with new-cut cedar branches.

"Mary, Mother of Jesus! It has to be the one Ben shot, I think!" Juan said, crossing himself.

"At least they took the time to put him in the ground." Ty was already heading toward the open gate.

"We traveling to Abilene now, Ty?" Juan queried obediently, as they hurried to the horses.

"I figure we go back north on the trail we come in on. Just maybe the marshal and Roy picked up a few of the cartridges and are coming our way. No telling, though, where the thieves are, but they won't be able to move real fast with that many horses. Abilene has to be where they are headed. We *are* goin' to Abilene, with or without the marshal and Roy.

The opening in the bulky storm clouds was closed now. Gray skies began to shroud the once-illuminated hill. They mounted quickly and galloped off toward the road to Abilene.

"Those riders are more exposed than in the past. It's got to be uncomfortable without the black of night to cover them. Total darkness is still a good two hours away," Ty remarked. "We will ride to the trail split. They went in two different directions with the horses. In my mind that's where we need to go first."

Riding rapidly, they made the trail split in less than two hours. When they arrived, Roy and the marshal were dismounted and staring at the ground. Roy was casually flipping a cartridge in his huge hand.

"Ty and me, we found where they held the stolen horses. We found a fresh grave, too," Juan announced proudly.

"They flew the coop! Abilene is the next stop for us," Ty said with determination.

Marshal Seward slipped into the saddle, moving close to Ty and Grey. "I'm sorry, Ty, Doc Diederich couldn't save Ben. We lost him. Doc fixed 'him so he didn't have no more pain."

Nothing more was said as the men started north into the rain. The sun was no longer visible. Only the hills all around were visible in the dying light of the day. Eventually, they stopped to rest and water the horses. The baying howls of nearby coyotes came and went. The marshal and Ty lit smokes while they waited. Roy put a fresh tobacco plug in his cheek and shed his slicker. True to his nature, Juan paced and fidgeted.

Ty broke the silence. "Ben saved my bacon many a time, in and out of the war. The man was all I had 'til I found Liz. Ain't many men like Ben. I'll miss him, that's for sure. Liz and little Ty won't know what to do with him not bein' there."

The marshal relit his curved stem pipe and reached into his pocket, retrieving a handful of cartridges. He handed them to Ty. "I'm a right good tracker, if I do say so myself. When we find these night thieves you may need these. A man can never tell when he might find them right handy." Instinctively, the four mounted, riding side by side through a grove of burr oaks and up a wide draw. Water from the hills streamed through on its way to a wide, rock-infested creek. "I've heard talk of a bigger-than-normal creek out this way. Might be Diamond Creek—or it might not," the marshal announced, to no one in particular.

Riding urgently now, they kept to the low ground. The rain continued to hold off, signaling it perhaps was done for the time being. Stopping in the dead of night to rest the horses, Ty laid out his thoughts.

"The way I see it, we need to split up somewhere south of the town."

Juan spoke up. "When I first rode to Abilene, I saw two roads that come in from the south. Cattle trails, for sure. I come in town on the widest. Surely, many smaller roads are around, but the horses could move much faster on the old, wide trails. We know these riders will be in a hurry, so I think they will surely choose one or the other."

"I figger we have less than three hours to get in front of the thieves. From here on, we make a fast ride. When we get near the old trails, they should be obvious, except it's still going to be dark, so Juan can point them out for us," Ty commanded. "The riders can't move near as fast as we can."

"The trails are no more than two miles from each other," Juan piped in.

"Roy, you and I will split off and stay put on the first road you come to. Juan and Austin, the other. If and when the riders come through, no reason whatsoever we can't follow at a distance," Ty reasoned, as he strapped on his gun belt from his saddlebag.

Juan whispered to Roy as they mounted. "Meester Ty is wearing big iron. When a much younger man, I seen him use it in Oklahoma. He put a bad man in the dirt before his gun cleared his holster."

Abilene

"If they ain't already come through, time is sure runnin' out on this here night. Don't imagine they's anxious to be in no daylight. No siree," Roy said, while carving off another plug of tobacco for his cheek. Grey and Roy's horse were hidden in a deep-wooded depression behind them. Both men sat concealed atop a hillock festooned with several wind-ravaged, thick bushes. "Might just be Lady Luck let these thieves down when Ben shot one of 'em. They's time when she don't play favorites. Makes a clean getaway for awhile, gets a body in a heap of dung."

"No doubt about that, Roy. We have all been victims," Ty said quickly.

Ty suspected Juan and the marshal were now hidden close to the trail that Juan suspected the night riders would use. He had not complained when Ty had made his choice of roads to watch.

"You hear something, Roy?" Ty asked.

"Sounds like a rider coming our way. He's in a real hurry," Roy said. Moments later, Juan appeared.

"That outfit come right by me and the marshal! Looked to be ten or twelve men pushing what looked to be seventy or eighty horses! I never seen the likes. The marshal, he is trailing behind them, and those riders is wasting no time."

Still in the saddle, Juan led them away. Behind their moving silhouettes, a sliver of pinkness appeared, signaling the welcome sunrise. They quickly discovered the marshal partially hidden in the first light, moving with caution through the thickets and trees bordering the old cattle trail. Barely visible in the distance, the stolen horses were seen moving swiftly toward the town. Ty rode up to the marshal's side.

"I'm thinkin', Marshal, we find out where their destination is, then settle in and wait. We might capture the whole kit and caboodle."

"We got like minds, Ty. Makes a heap of sense. Ain't nothing that would please me more than to find out who's buying the rides. One thing's for sure: whoever it is, they got plenty a money to buy more than a year's worth of stolen horses. Ain't none of 'em been nags, neither."

Juan had his field glasses in his hand as he joined in, "The men, they are moving the horses off the trail. I see this now. When I was here before, I remember a deep valley south of the town. They are moving in that direction. I did not go there, though. But I saw it from a distance when I returned home."

The four of them watched intently from the surrounding deep woods while the night riders led the stolen horses down a steep and long incline, past a handsome ranch house, and on into the heart of the tree-surrounded valley. Dozens of horses were milling about as the stolen horses worked their way down the steep entrance to a massive corral. A lone, tall hand waved the men and horses through the gate he held open. The morning light had just begun to envelop the hidden valley. They watched while the riders talked briefly with the man and then trotted off up the long hill.

"You best follow those boys, Roy," the marshal ordered.

"It will sure be a pleasure. Yes, it will," Roy said.

"If for some reason you suspect them devils is fixin' to leave or go down that trail again, one of us for sure will be around here close, so hightail it back. We need to figure out what to do if they are plannin' on disappearin'."

"They ain't getting out of my sight, Marshal."

Ty nodded as Roy started to depart. "One of us will be close to the telegraph office at sundown tonight, so's you can report what's happening, if anything."

Throughout the new day, most of the rain clouds had dispersed, giving way to a fine afternoon. Juan and Ty, along with the marshal, watched intently as other interested hands appeared at the corral, talking and gesturing toward one horse then another.

"Seems there's a heap of admiring going on down below, Ty. Your remuda is got 'em all worked up. They had to have seen them before at the races. Those horses plain lured them thieves like bees to honey. The bait's been swallered."

"Looks like it, Marshal. It sure does. Wonder what's their next move. Seems it would be a good idea to move soon. Unless, for some reason, they decided they are plumb safe right here. Then again, they might just be confident they gave anyone trailing them the slip. Nobody we seen so far seems to be in no hurry."

"I don't buy it none, because of the way the raid was so well planned. This bunch has themselves a careful leader. He ain't no common horse thief."

Sundown sent Juan to Abilene, where he located Roy lounging behind a little telegraph structure. "I ain't starvin' no more," he said when Juan joined him. "Want some tortillas? They's in my saddlebag if'n you're hankerin' to eat. Found a little lean-to just off the street, down near the cattle pens. An old man was makin' burritos, chili, and fajitas. Had a young girl helping him. Told me I was his last customer for the day. Weren't nobody else around. I bought what would travel and put it in my bags. He even wrapped what I bought in newspapers. Chili don't travel, so I ate it all myself."

Juan retrieved a tortilla. "You seen any of the riders?"

"Shore did. Five went into that dancehall on that there corner. Can't be certain, but I think one of 'em was that jingle-bob loud one Hammer pointed out to us at the races. It was getting dark, but I'd bet my bottom dollar it was him. He was doin' all the talkin'. Paying no attention to anything but hisself. They been in there awhile. I think the others musta stayed somewhere close to them rides. They didn't come in town, noways."

When Roy returned to the hidden valley, he found the marshal sleeping soundly. Ty was seated close by.

"Them five riders was all I seen in town. Didn't see no more, Ty." Roy handed the food to him and sat down. "Juan will keep watch this morning. Them saloons is doing a land-office business, that's for damn sure. I found a place out of the bustle, where a man can go for some vittles."

Ty woke the marshal, handing him some food. Both men ate hungrily. The night was clear and warm. A high, star-filled sky hung above the valley. Roy pulled the saddle off his horse. Finding a good spot, he laid down against his saddle and nodded off in no time.

"No tellin' what tomorrow will bring, Ty. Why don't you get some shut-eye. I'll keep an eye out. Visibility ain't no problem on a night like this. Besides, I got Juan's glasses."

"I was thinkin' that myself, Marshal," Ty declared, making himself comfortable under a tall sycamore. An ample prairie wind held the ever-present insects at bay. The quiet night soon grew into an equally pleasant sunrise.

"Ain't been no activity down at the corral," the marshal confirmed when Ty stirred awake at first light. "Only thing I seen other than the horses was a passel of deer and more turkeys than I could count. Not a sign of a hand keeping watch on them rides or nothing. Roy's on his way to find

Juan. He is fixin' to watch through the better part of the day. Juan will be bringing coffee soon."

Shortly, Juan appeared with two canteens of coffee and water along with a bag of warm tortillas. Jagged darts of sunlight fed themselves through the leaves of the tall trees, spreading uneven traces of light on the quiet valley.

"The riders, they was plenty drunk when they come out of the dancehall. Some senoritas was with them, too. An old house behind another saloon is where they spent the night. Up close, I saw a one-armed man go after the gringos. He locked the doors. Then he, too, went toward the old house alone. I seen no sign of these men before I come back this way. I didn't see nobody, neither, near the marshal's office."

Finally awake, Ty splashed water from a canteen into his hands and washed his face. Then he poured himself a generous cup of warm coffee. The marshal seemed to be getting impatient. "I'm beginnin' to think that this outfit might just decide to lay low. Just let the horses be for the time being."

"No doubt that's one trail to follow," Ty answered. "To my mind, Austin, that might be a stretch, bein' this bunch has been so careful up to this here point. If nothing changes today, though, you could be right. One thing for sure: we ain't goin' to be perched up here much longer. It's getting us nowhere at all. We all sorta agreed the train is a powerful possibility for moving them horses. We need to find out just when the next one is due to arrive."

Darkness had set in when the marshal and Ty rode into town, carefully avoiding the main road and staying in the shadows. Relieving Roy, Ty remained out of sight with the horses while the marshal walked behind the main-street structures on his way to the train station. A lone, dim light in a round fixture illuminated the door. Beside it was the Kansas Pacific schedule displayed in a rectangular glass window. The next train was due to arrive at noon the following day. It was headed to points west, with two passenger cars accompanying sufficient livestock cars to empty the pens. The ticket agent inside did not notice him.

"I don't suppose it would hurt nothing if you or myself night ride near the tracks while the other stays around here," the marshal proposed when he returned from the station.

"Why not, Marshal. If things is this quiet tomorrow, maybe we could find an ideal place to hold the train up!" Ty said jokingly.

"That ain't exactly funny. Especially coming from an ex-ranger.

"I guess you're right, Austin, but your sense of humor is severely lackin'."

"I ain't had no humor in me ever since Elvira booted me out of my house," the sullen marshal admitted.

"When I get back here, have a plan all mapped out on just how we can pull it all off," Ty said, trotting off in the distance.

When he returned hours later, Ty found the marshal had hardly moved from where he had left him. Sitting down next to his dejected friend, he bit off the end of a smoke and lit it. "You ever rode that train, Marshal?"

"Nope. Never."

"Well, if you had you might have noticed those tracks could have gone straight as an arrow, 'cause it's flat as a pancake west of here. But it don't. Instead of stayin' straight, three miles west of here, it leaves the flat ground and dips down a long hill, veers left, and then there's a stretch where tall timber and low mounds is on both sides. Seems almost like whoever ramrodded them rail crews had a serious case of drunk goin' on, or he wanted the passengers to go about viewing the last trees they will see 'til they get to Colorado. Then I found something that was just as hard to make sense to me. So I took a real good look-see."

"What was it you seen?"

"An oversized loading ramp come up adjacent to the tracks. Right out of the woods. Soon after the ramp, the tracks make another slow turn back toward the flatland, as if the boss suddenly got over being drunk. I mulled it all over as I rode back to here. Two facts finally jumped out at me."

"Two facts?"

"Two facts. Well, looking at the turn back towards the flatland, I realized the front of the train, where most of the passenger cars are located, don't have a view of the end cars, 'cause of the timber and curve. Fact one. Then there was something about that downhill curve that set me to scratching my head—even more than a loading ramp sitting close to nothing at all. Fact two: the downhill stretch in the woods has to be near the west boundary of that hidden valley we been scoutin'. Some hombre with real authority figured if they had a notion to load some livestock, it could quickly be accomplished without folks asking no questions or even seein' the loadin' process. Did you eyeball that gate in the corral opposite where the horses was led through?"

"I did indeed," the marshal responded.

"Well, I'm thinking it opens onto a direct path to that loadin' ramp, as sure as you and me are standing in the dark. Coming back, I kept to the tracks, and when me and Grey went behind the station, I noticed what looked like a body having some trouble standing up. It was an old man who had gotten himself all liquored up. My guess is, he is hoping to hitch a ride on the train expected tomorrow. He mumbled something about Abilene didn't suit his style no more. Said he used to ride with old Jesse Chisholm in the early drives to Abilene until he got busted up in a stampede. Been living here ever since, doin' odd jobs. I had a little coffee left in my canteen, so I gave him some. It sort of perked the feller up. Don't know why, but I inquired about that spread we been keepin' our eyes on. Seems hardly none of the townsfolk is welcome on the place. Accordin' to the old codger, the place is owned by a railroad man that goes by the name of Clifford, if I heard him right. He was mixin' up words on account of the liquor. 'Cole Clifford' was the handle I come up with. A railroad bossman from back east."

"Abilene got themselves a new sheriff a ways back. We ain't met him. Maybe a visit to his office in the morning might make some sense. Come to think of it, Juan sent us a wire stating that Clifford name when he was nosing around back when," the marshal said while he relit his ever-present pipe. "Might be some kind of connection, I suppose, Ty."

"Ain't no sense to stay the night. I have a notion them horses is supposed to be loaded tomorrow. Ain't nobody of interest is going to be in Abilene itself. Seems them boys is likely to be in the timber, waiting on a train."

"Buzzin' around in my head is the notion, 'why would a well-to-do feller, say this Clifford Cole, get hisself all tied up in the horse-thieving trade,'" Ty wondered aloud as they rode off to join Roy and Juan. Once there, in the waning darkness, they discovered both men talking quietly and sharing some cold coffee. Soon, the exhausted marshal propped himself up against a big cottonwood and began to snore loudly.

"Meester Ty, on my scouting trips, it seemed this hombre Clifford was said to be no friend to none of the citizens. His men, they done some bad things. It is said there has been gunplay."

Sometime after Juan had set off to fetch some food, Ty awakened to a building, warm wind beneath feathery white clouds that appeared as if painted on the sky. In the short time that Juan had taken to find coffee and corncakes, Ty's developing plan had gained considerable traction in his mind. His concentration seemed to be most evident in the fact that any conversation from him had disappeared. Ty had cleared sticks and dead leaves away and commenced to draw in the dirt. All the while, he murmured to himself as if he was all alone.

"Roy, this is as good a time as any to make an acquaintance with the new sheriff. Why don't you see if he might be available for some conversation? Might do well to let it out you been deputized by US Marshal Seward. Find out if you can discover where his credentials come from. Let on you sorta stumbled past the Clifford spread by accident. Say how fine it was to your eye. Size him up so to speak. Tell him you come to Abilene to meet someone on the train. His place of business is next to the wagon shop, if you hadn't noticed."

Later, morning hot winds rode with Roy's return. Jail's plumb full," he said matter-of-factly, while retreating to the ample shade hiding the men. "Says he was a drover 'cause he come from longhorn people. Then found hisself in Fremont, Nebraska. Worked as a deputy then moved on to St. Joe and Sedalia, Missouri, until the longhorns was banned. Spent a few months in the war. Come from Westport to Abilene."

"What does he call himself?" Ty asked.

"Chuck Goodnight. Don't seem like the kind of fella you'd want to get on his wrong side."

"If he is who he says he is his granddaddy was sure familiar with the law. Both ends," the marshal threw in. "Met that old devil once myself. Ain't no man drove a harder bargain nowhere. Charlie's oldest boy was killed in a gunfight down in Coffeyville."

Chapter 36

High-Dollar Bargain

"You and me been conducting horse business for a good while now; I reckon it's only right to disclose my intentions regarding any future deliveries: don't expect none. My men is expressin' a strong interest in scattering to the winds. One of my boys got himself shot just two days back. We was gathering this here delivery. Some is the finest horses I have ever set my eyes on in the tallgrass country. I'll be going into the ranching business," Sim announced.

"Congratulations, Mr. Collins. I'm fond of the business myself. Just east of Abilene, I'm raising fifteen hundred head of cattle," Cole Clifford said proudly. "However, horses remain in my favor. Particularly horses such as those in my corral at this time. I've seen no finer."

Next to Sim, Peak and Dusty Nelson sat quietly, watching the strained conversation. Two of the ranch hands stood nearby, seeming to watch nothing in particular. "I'll be taking my cattle up the Oregon Trail soon. Of course, I'll be needing a no-nonsense man to represent my interests once they reach Montana. A new market often can be rewarding. I don't suppose you'd be interested?"

Peak and Dusty watched Sim shift nervously in his chair while he brewed up his answer. "Mr. Clifford, like I said, my intention is staying in Kansas. Most of the men and their horses is going to be on the train. Trailing cattle just ain't our specialty. 'Preciate the offer, nonetheless. Might as well settle up now. Then we'll be moving on."

"Certainly, as an enterprising individual, I don't blame you. I have made quite an investment in your business. My particular customers are very impressed."

Handing Sim a thick envelope, Clifford watched carefully as the bills were counted twice. "I'm curious, Mr. Collins, if you have made many acquaintances since you began the horse-delivery enterprise?"

Sim looked at the smiling Clifford. He understood the railroader's inquiry quite clearly. "Just my men. Reckon I ain't been seen otherwise. Being careful is my true nature."

"Nobody understands that fact more than me, Sim. However, you sure stand out in a crowd. Pardon me for inquiring, but that bandana that covers your forehead is quite noticeable. Never seen you without it. Did you have some kind of injury?"

"Bull Run left a mark on me. I aim to get it tended to soon. You have a problem with it?" Sim inquired angrily.

Dusty and Peak suddenly grew alert. The conversation seemed headed downhill.

"I meant nothing disparaging, Collins. Only that you would be easy to remember. Awhile ago, you might recall, when we first did business, we set up an evening in town. You and your men set about raisin' hell and whoring. Of course, in *this* town, there was hundreds intent on doing the same thing. This town is full of desperate and unruly men. Until recently, the law around here has been severely lacking. But now two of my men are stuck in jail. That hasn't occurred in the past. I suppose the new sheriff is seeking to make a name for himself by taking such liberties. Surely, Collins, you can understand how any connection between the two of us might cause some unwanted problems. Honestly, I admit your desire to remain in Kansas causes me uneasiness."

"It's no use, Mr. Clifford. I'll be putting down stakes in the tallgrass as a law-abiding citizen. I'll not be answering to no man. Putting in with your enterprise don't interest me none."

"I had hoped you would not take offense. Furthermore I am prepared to provide ample incentive for you and several of your men. I'd hoped you would hear me out."

Peak and Dusty seemed to have calmed the uneasiness. Unexpectedly, Dusty interjected. "Boss, what's it hurt to listen to Mr. Clifford's offer?"

"You ain't gonna change my mind no way, but I reckon I'll hear you through," Sim said grudgingly.

"It won't take long, Collins. I suppose you don't mind your men listening in?"

Sim took stock of Peak's face, wishing he hadn't brought him along. Zeb would have been a better choice.

"I reckon not. It won't bother me none," he lied.

"The long and short of my situation is this: My cattle operation has been one where I been receiving steers in the same manner as those horses. As my railroad moves west, the law seems to be following right behind, which makes doing business ... somewhat more difficult, shall we say. Shifting my business farther west, where it is less crowded, is what I am planning for the near future. Men like yourself will be needed; men who can lead, bargain, and handle themselves. I am more inclined to receive livestock than raise them. Although I have done some raising on occasion, it's been far more rewarding to hold down my costs by simply having good men like yourself bring these animals to me at a reasonable price."

Sim watched as Cole Clifford reached into his vest pocket, pulling out yet another envelope with his name embossed it. He handed it to Sim.

"Count it. It is all yours if you agree to leave the tallgrass country with a handful of your boys. Ten thousand dollars buys a lot of land west of Abilene."

Sim fingered the cash. The conflict inside him began to boil. He tried to imagine how much land the money would buy him. Retrieving the seventeen thousand from the heist back in Raton plus a year and a half of horse money from the raids coupled with the bills in his hand would allow him to secure a huge spread. Dusty and Zeb, with one or two more of his men, would be all he needed to run his gentleman's spread.

Cole Clifford sat patiently waiting for Sim's reply.

"This offer is tempting I'll admit, Cole. You've been a straight shooter all along. We ain't had no problems, you and me. But I got a question or two stuck in my craw."

"What might they be?"

"Well, I been wondering all along why a rich fella like yourself would be in the receivin' business in the first place?"

"That *is* a question I suppose I would ask myself if *I* was in your boots," Cole Clifford answered calmly.

"Ownin' part of a railroad and such, it don't make no sense to my way of reasonin' why you would take such risks."

"I trust you, Collins, or I wouldn't be making this offer. The short of it is, I do not quite own the Kansas Pacific Railroad just yet. The long of it is, I have an obligation to my father-in-law's estate. May he rest in peace. Then, nearly one year ago, I lost my wife. My banker in Kansas City is demanding his money by the end of next year. Shall I say, there is a real need to supplement my income, or the loan will be recalled, and then I lose the opportunity to own the railroad. The cattle have a ready market up the Oregon Trail. Buyers of my horses have need of good horseflesh below the Mexican border. The traveling shows out toward California way purchase some fine horses at top prices, and they don't ask questions. In the future, I will remove myself from the receiving business, if and when I pay the loan in Kansas City. A man like you could help me speed up things."

Peak and Dusty listened with great interest while Clifford's two men seemed to pay little or no mind.

"I am a very careful man, Collins. Word came to me you are wanted in Texas. Also, several killings have taken place in the tallgrass country recently—and in Oklahoma, during horse-stealing raids. An enterprising man like you would do well to make himself scarce around these parts."

"Ain't nobody can hogtie my outfit to any of them raids," Sim said seriously, pointing a finger toward Peak and Dusty.

"Perhaps not, but these kind of raids are no everyday occurrence. You're smart, Collins. You have to worry about the killings, because it causes the law to search for who did the shootings," Clifford replied. "There are times when they don't seem to give up on the hunt. Our new sheriff in Abilene comes from Texas hard stock. He's bent on making a name for himself any way he can."

"Plenty of years have done passed without any trouble with no lawman. They don't scare me none," Sim snapped bitterly.

Cole Clifford pulled his pocket watch from his vest. "Seems we will be loading the new horses in less than two hours. I have stated my case as best I could. I have railroad business to attend to now, prior to the train arriving. What is your answer? I'll wait no longer, Sim Collins."

Sim shifted uneasily in his chair. Booming, hot winds blew through the windows. The heat in the room had become close to unbearable. The embossed envelope in his hand was becoming damp. Salty sweat came down his face from under the bandana that hid his branded forehead.

"I reckon a setup like you described don't come by every day, Cole. Bein' my outfit is going all different directions tomorrow, I will accept your offer."

"Fine, Collins! Fine! I suppose you will want to settle up with your men right away. It's time for me to get along towards town. You won't regret your change in plans. Not one bit." Cole shook Sim's hand before he departed.

Once outside the ranch house, Sim and his men were met with boiling, strong winds. "It's hotter than the kitchens of Hades," Peak complained, as they made their way towards the oversized corral. "You might as well know I ain't gonna work for you or the railroad man," he said loudly.

"No offer was coming your way, no how, Peak," Sim said coldly.

Quickly, Dusty stepped between them.

"You just leavin' Jake to die didn't sit well with me, Sim. It weren't right."

"Your opinion don't mean nothing to me, Peak. You best be on your way to Kansas City. It's too hot to shoot you today."

Dusty hustled Peak away from Sim, leaving him to ponder his unexpected commitment to Cole Clifford. No matter the situation, it seemed Sim was destined to be rich and, perhaps, very difficult to find.

Chapter 32

Hot Wind Capture

"There can't be more'n a handful of passengers boarding that train. If it *is* on schedule, I figger loading that pen of 'horns I seen won't take more than an hour. Another ten minutes to get under way toward the big bend in the timber puts that train around two-thirty alongside that doggone ramp," the marshal speculated.

"I reckon that is about how *I* see it, too. If we see them riders come through that gate yonder, we will make our move," replied Ty. "Since we agree it's a mite too soon for a new sheriff to be beholden to any special folks, he deserves to be warned about our intentions. Added complications wouldn't be no good at all. *Especially* since it wouldn't be no problem to confuse our intention for stoppin' a train run by Abilene's railroad boss."

"We ain't got no warrants for any arrests neither, Ty. If I can round up the sheriff, I'll see he's not left out in the dark. Come to think of it, we don't even have no names we can give that sheriff. I reckon it don't matter none, though. We have to stop this whole affair now, one way or another. Today is as good a time as any to take my first train ride, too."

Amid the thickest of trees and shade, the three of them watched the marshal lope off in the stifling, hot winds of the day. Even their carefully selected lookout offered little relief from the swirling blasts of heat.

After a time, Juan broke the silence. "Men are moving inside the corral now! Maybe a dozen of them. I recognize some of the riders that come with the horses for sure. It is my hope the man you had me send for is on his way, Meester Ty. He'll be needed, for sure."

When the marshal trotted into town, he rode straight down Broadway, the main street. The mid-day hot winds had driven Abilene's citizens off the streets in search of relief from the heat. At the sheriff's clapboard office, he was greeted by broad-brimmed man of average size. He seemed too mild-eyed for a lawman.

"I'm sure delighted to make your acquaintance, Marshal. Have a seat," he said with a toothy, wide grin. "Cigar? A cigar seller's been in town for two days. Damn good ones if you buy the top-dollar offerings." Myself, that's all I smoke."

The marshal accepted the cigar, sticking it in his sweat-soaked shirt. "I come here on business. Serious business, Sheriff."

"Name's Goodnight. Mostly, folks call me 'Kinch.' Old Charles Goodnight is my uncle," he revealed proudly.

"Ain't no name in these parts any larger than Good-night," the marshal responded.

Following a short discussion, he prepared to leave for the train station to purchase his ticket. "You can count on me bein' at the party, Marshal. All I done since I got here two months ago is herding drunk stockmen into this here jail. They get all lit up on that Kansas sheep dip then end up in the tenderloin district in the south part of town. Two nights back it got ugly when one of them ladies of the night got messed up real bad. She damned near bled to death." He paused to let that thought settle, then continued on. "Horse thieves where I come from in Concho County, Texas, is just about died out. Most been hung. Especially if the horses was owned by Oliver Loving, John Chisholm, or old Charlie. If you was a lawman in Oklahoma or Texas, a name like Ty McCord rings a bell. It will be a downright pleasure to lend a hand to the two of you boys."

" Marshal, I reckon you will be one of the first to see Mr. Cole Clifford's private car when the train arrives," said the ticket clerk inside the station. "I hear from Kansas City it is right fine, indeed. 'Course, the regular passengers like yourself ain't about to see *inside*. Folks say it's got all velvet-covered furniture, and it even has a bed! It's all done in dark wood, with a space where Mr. Clifford's choice wine is supposedly stored. Don't that just beat all!"

The excited clerk handed the marshal his ticket. The marshal seated himself next to a portly woman with an oversized suitcase. She was waving her fan frantically in a losing effort to gain relief from the sweat-lodge conditions.

"Land of Goshen," she gasped while mopping her immense forehead with her free hand. "Can't imagine ever returning to this godforsaken land. No, sir. I'll never come back."

The marshal's thoughts were of more important matters. Could he trust a sheriff he had met less than an hour ago? Nothing would prevent him from warning Abilene's most famous citizen of the day. A most troubling unknown it was.

The idea of the sheriff's presence in the plan continued to gnaw at him as he boarded the train. He selected a seat directly behind the shiny, new car that belonged to Cole Clifford. The oversized clock in the station had read ten minutes after two. The ride to the bend in the timber would be short. From then on, things promised to be dangerously uncertain.

Ty, Roy, and Juan were now concealed in the thick, deep, overcrowded woods surrounding the loading ramp at the end of the trail between it and the deep-valley corral.

They watched quietly as a lone, unexpected rider slowly rode beside the tracks until eventually disappearing down into a deep depression in the trees. Patiently, they waited in the overwhelming heat for the sound of the approaching train, wondering what the rider's intentions were.

Roy was cradling his scattergun in his huge arms when he spoke in a whisper to Ty and Juan. "You reckon this here Clifford fellow is gonna have some help riding on the train? 'Course ain't no way to tell. If'n they is, we gonna be a bit shorthanded."

"It's a good bet most of his help is in that corral, fixin' to load the horses. Could be it would make sense some would ride on from here on the train. That way, no prying eyes could complicate things," Ty said. "Then they could just get the hell out of Abilene."

Juan scurried away for a quick look at the horses and returned hurriedly. "I count a dozen men. Three are not armed. The others, they are for certain. It would be very good if the message I sent to Rockdale arrived in your friend's hand, Meester Ty."

"It sure wouldn't hurt none, Juan. He'd be right handy if things get real dicey."

After what seemed like an eternity, a lonely whistle signaling the train's departure from Abilene alerted the concealed lawmen to their task at hand. The chugging, iron monster came into view within a few minutes, slowly progressing toward the inclined turn. Behind the engine was a large green-and-red car sporting bright lettering. Oversized windows afforded those inside a wide view of the surroundings. Once the engine reached the upslope, the brakes ground the wheels to a screeching halt. The doors of three cattle cars near the end of the train had been left open wide for the quick loading procedure that was to come.

With Juan and Roy out of view on the opposite side of the trail, Ty watched as the first horses were spirited, three abreast, through the wide gate toward the waiting train. Several were quickly identified from his remuda. They were led by a stocky rider sitting tall in the saddle. He wore a bright bandana over his forehead and under his hat. His horse was of fine breeding. Several more young riders followed, urging the string along with whistles and shouts. Forty stolen horses paraded down the trail. Another rider brought up the tail end of the string. Quickly and efficiently the horses climbed up the ramp and into the waiting cars, then the process was repeated until eighty-three were loaded. Finally, the leader with the bright bandana scrambled up the steps to the bright, fancy car behind the engine and disappeared quickly within.

Ty concluded the bright car had to be the property of the receiver of the horses—one Cole Clifford, railroad boss. A man who could easily move stolen livestock anywhere he pleased. The unsuspecting riders dismounted and were casually moving about the empty loading ramp. It was time to call a halt to the proceedings.

Unexpectedly, the lone rider they had observed earlier appeared from out of the timber. As he approached closer, Ty could see a flash of sunlight off the badge he was wearing. The sheriff! Conversation stopped as the alerted riders watched nervously while the sheriff peered through the open slats of the rail cars. He was taking his time. Then he sauntered up to the engine and climbed inside.

Moments later a tall, well-attired Cole Clifford, along with the bandana-wearing man, emerged from the bright-colored car. When they appeared, Ty noticed Marshal Seward stepping down from the passenger car behind. Clifford and the lead rider continued to walk quickly toward the engine.

"Why in tarnation are we not underway?" Clifford hollered loudly. "What is going on?"

Suddenly, the riders began to scramble as they saw

the marshal draw his pistol. Clifford and the lead rider spun around, only to see the marshal pointing his weapon directly at them.

" Have you gone haywire mister? "

"I am a US Marshal. I've come to arrest you and these men for horse thievery, Mr. Clifford. I have plenty of help around," he proclaimed through his lying teeth. Instantly, a shot rang out from among the riders. It slammed into the marshal's hip, sending him awkwardly down on the rails. The gun flew out of his hand behind him. Sheriff Goodnight jumped down from the engine just in time to see Sim Collins draw from his holster. Confusion ran roughshod over the goings on. As Roy and Juan raced to the scene, two of the riders lurched for their horses. Roy sent a loud blast over their heads from his scatter shotgun. This abruptly stopped their escape attempt. Cole Clifford seemed to stagger for a moment, then he fell into Sim causing his shot at the sheriff to divert into the ground.

Out of the confusion, Zeb Hernandez was able to mount his ride and make a mad dash toward the corral. He shouted all the way. Juan blew him out of his saddle with two shots to the chest, yelling "Adios, amigo!" More shots glanced off of the engine car, forcing the sheriff back inside. Unhurt, Sim and Peak jumped between the engine and the private car, running desperately down the tracks. The sheriff left the safety of the engine when he saw they were getting away. In hot pursuit, the sheriff's searing bullet tore into Sim's shoulder. It momentarily stopped him. Chaos reigned supreme.

Running toward the scene, Ty saw Cole Clifford jump to his feet and retrieve a pistol from inside his coat. He leveled it directly toward the marshal, still prone on the tracks. Ty's quick shot from his peacemaker slammed into Clifford's arm and sent the man's pistol to the ground. Able-bodied but panicked riders raced through the woods on foot.

In the woods, Roy's scattergun roared once more, sending a tall thief to his knees. Ty sprinted toward the wounded marshal. "Don't shoot me!" Cole Clifford pleaded, while raising his bloody hands. Ty hesitated just long enough to smash his fist into Clifford's face, shattering his nose and cheek. A terrified eyeball protruded from its socket. The blow sent him tumbling into a bloody heap.

Desperate to locate young Sheriff Goodnight, Ty ran the length of the train and found him sitting beneath the last of the cattle cars. "It's my leg. I can't walk! They shot me before I could get at 'em!" Anxiously, he motioned toward the cars containing the riled-up horses. "Look out, McCord!" the sheriff yelled.

Instinctively, Ty wheeled around. A few yards behind him, a one-armed man appeared seemingly from out of nowhere. Drawing his long pistol from a shoulder holster, the one-armed man hesitated for a second. A sudden, hair-raising screech from Juan had diverted his attention. It was long enough for the sheriff's Colt to send its hot lead through the man's forehead. He crumpled to the ground, face first.

Momentarily, the shouts and noises of the fracas seemed to cease all at once. Juan joined Ty, cautiously peering inside the horse cars for any sign of a man's worn boots among the horses. Unsuccessful, they paused for Ty to thumb cartridges into his peacemaker. Juan then proceeded to enter one of the passenger cars.

"Odd," Ty mused. "Not a single passenger has come out of these cars."

While Ty pondered the situation, a heavy, wide door slid open on the far side of one of the horse cars. Horses came spilling out, dashing madly in all directions. Some briefly stumbled, but the black-and-white pinto the hatless rider rode did not. He clung frantically to the flowing mane of the wild-eyed mare, flying into the trees and quickly disappearing. Dusty Nelson would regain his precious freedom on this hot, deadly day. He was never seen again in the Kansas prairie.

Momentarily, Juan reappeared from the first-in-line passenger car. "Two riders were once inside this car. One was the snake-face thief Hammer pointed out to us at the races. Holy Mother of Jesus! It's hotter than Maria's oven!" Juan said, mopping his face. "Very frightened, they are. It seems in all the commotion, the fear of being shot kept them inside.

"Well, then—you see about the marshal, while I take a gander in the next car," Ty ordered.

He looked carefully at the six seated, frightened passengers. One large lady in a long dress was crying hysterically and fanning herself with all her might. The others sat, unmoving, until he made his swift exit. The last car contained only two harmless old men. Both held thick Bibles in their laps.

"One of us, or Sheriff Goodnight, surely would have spotted them two riders if they had been in the open anywhere near this train." Juan shook his head in agreement.

"Me and Juan for *sure* would have seen a man, had he been on top of these here cars," Roy added.

"The rest of the horses are sufferin' something awful. We'd best see to that soon. Make sure the sheriff ain't where he can get hisself trampled. Abilene has plenty of drovers to help round up the horses later. Some of those boys might just be sober by this time of day."

Juan scampered off but quickly returned. "The sheriff vamoosed, Meester Ty. Only the blood stains remain!"

Ty thought for an instant. "I figure it ain't likely he has got snagged in a hostage situation, for they'd be showin' him to us by now. I suppose the sheriff could be dead, but something tells me that's likely not the case." Ty considered the unlikely prospect of the two night raiders having slithered through the trap and disappearing. "I have this powerful notion them two night-ridin' thieves is slow roasting inside one of these horse cars. Don't seem likely finding themselves in one of them cattle cars. Wouldn't make a lick of sense. 'Horns in tight confines is a mite dangerous. One wrong move, and a man might find one of them horns stuck clean through him."

"Time's come to let the horses loose, Juan. Open up the doors."

Reluctant only for an instant, the horses charged through the opening, onto the loading ramp, and into the trees, with some racing back down the trail from which they had come, winding up in the deep-valley corral so carefully constructed by Cole Clifford.

Near the center of the escaping horses, two riders were barely seen, clinging Indian style to the sides of a fine roan mare and a pale, palomino stallion from Ty's remuda. Ty and Juan held their fire. Running wildly behind the escaping riders, Juan found his filly and leaped into the saddle. An instant later, Ty thundered past him on his gray brute.

Barely visible in the distance, the two riders, now upright on their horses, tore through brush and thickets, breaking into a wide clearing. Grey was quickly narrowing the distance between them. Juan's filly strained to keep pace, but the brute thundering away toward the riders was too much horse. Juan knew for sure Ty would not risk an errant shot that might injure one of his prize horses. The big, determined ranger was close enough to see a bright bandana on one of the escaping thieves. The leader!

A few strides behind the leader, a thin thief reached for his sidearm and triggered a wild shot at his pursuers. The fleeing thieves splashed through a narrow, shallow stream, racing to the opposite bank before flying off in opposite directions. Ty gestured to Juan for him to pursue the roan with its thin rider.

Dead ahead were thick, crowded cedars and spreading

hedge, obscuring a narrow animal trail. Blistered leaves of tall sycamores hung from above. Both the desperate thief and his horse plunged into the denseness and disappeared from sight. Juan stopped his pursuit long enough to glance over his shoulder, catching a glimpse of Ty and Grey threading their way through the woods some distance away. Juan drew his pistol, cautiously proceeding into the threatening, furnace-like confines before him. His white-footed filly's hooves sounded as loud as church bells. He was enveloped in sweat that streamed down his dark face. The Colt in his hand seemed too heavy, its grip too wet and slick.

Prairie-dog mounds dotted the narrow trail. Without warning, the filly suddenly stopped in her tracks. Her ears popped up with the desperate sounds of an injured and frightened horse. Ty's roan was down nearby! Where was the rider? Close for certain. Juan's frayed nerves were on edge. Dismounting, Juan led his alerted filly toward the dreadful sounds. Ty's mare lay on her side in bulging-eyed agony. A jagged bone had pierced the skin above her ankle. Not hesitating, Juan triggered a shot that quickly ended her misery—and revealed his vulnerable location.

Peak sat hidden just far enough away not be detected by the little Mexican. He had been pitched on top of a low, jagged stump when his horse had stepped in a prairie-dog hole. With each breath, searing pain in his ribs reeked havoc on his consciousness. His survival would depend on his capturing the pursuer's horse.

Peak reasoned that if Sim did escape, he would return to the safety of their hidden corral. Little Jake Quinlan was buried there, and so would Sim Collins be, if somehow Peak could climb into the saddle on the Mex's ride. Sim's money belt—all of it!—would then be his property.

The prospect of seeing the end of Sim Collins's life sustained him as he rose on unsteady feet. Thankfully, his twin, black-handled pistols still hung securely by his side. He labored to breathe in the thick, hot air about him. Suddenly, an unbearable pain shot through his body an instant before a river of blood flowed from his gaping mouth. Vainly, he attempted to stem the tide with his hands, but it was a lost cause. Rivulets escaped between his fingers and down his blood-soaked shirt, finally dripping onto the parched earth at his feet.

Before returning to the train, dragging the dead rider and tying him onto his little horse proved to be a mighty struggle for Juan. The long, hot walk back to the waiting train loomed before him. Several scorching hours went by before he finally arrived.

Miles to the south of Abilene, Sim Collins had somehow cleverly eluded the determined tallgrass ranger.

Ty stood atop a tall, barren hill, peering through his field glasses. "He's desperate, and he's surely not much ahead of us, Grey. Me being him, I reckon I'd lay low 'til dark. At the nearest spread, I'd commence to find a saddle and fresh horse. Ain't many choices out here. Anyhow, workin' at night is familiar to him. Seems there is slim chance he would choose to circle back towards Abilene specially in these wide-open areas where we can see for miles. Besides he's been shot. Grey, best you see to it we find the nearest ranch. I figure we play our hand there."

Unrelenting heat still accompanied them as the two worked their way down the rocky, oblong path. Following a considerable ride, a herd of longhorns made an appearance in a pasture slanted between several low and barren hillocks. A stone ranch house sat at the foot of the most vertical of the mounds, an ageless attempt to shelter man from the ravages of harsh conditions. Several drowsy horses in the corral watched lazily as Ty and Grey sauntered by. The place was well tended to.

Ty hitched Grey, then proceeded to knock determinedly on the heavy, ranch house door. A stooped over, wind-burned, old rancher came to the door. In one hand, he supported himself with a sturdy, carved wooden cane with a big knob on the end. The rancher took swift notice of the big iron on Ty's hip.

"State your business out here in no man's land," the crusty rancher demanded gruffly. "You a lawman? I ain't seen one in a year or two. He was as black as Mississippi mud. Said he'd been deputized by some yahoo down in Wichita—with the handle of Earp. What kind of godforsaken name is that?"

"Seems Earp drummed up quite a reputation for himself awhile back," Ty said honestly. "As for me, I've made a home in the tallgrass. Got a wife and little boy. Could say I'm doin' part-time deputy work for Marshal Austin Seward, headquartered in Tanglewood. My spread is a short ways from Beezer. Name's McCord."

"You claim a first name?"

"Most call me Ty."

"You don't strike me as no deputy."

"Ain't much I can do about your opinion. My day was spent trailin' a horse thief. Seems he's dead set against making my acquaintance. He might be headin' this here direction. The hombre is downright handy at stealin' and he's a slick one. That horse he's on is bound to be plumb tuckered out by now. Ridin' bareback, I figure he's cravin' a saddle to cinch on a fresh horse."

"Seems like yesterday I come out in this country. There wasn't no concerns about horse thieves way out here. I was born in Kentucky. Name's Shean, McCord. C. G. Shean. When I was a young fellow and half crazy, I worked the early days of the Santa Fe Trail, trail markin' between Round Narrows down to Santa Fe and Taos. Met Jed Smith when he come down the trail. Now *there* was a man!"

Yellow light from a low sun shown through a window, highlighting the talkative old rancher's wrinkled face. "There's a trickle of water in a ravine over yonder. Can't see it from here, but it ain't far at all. Any rider worth his salt will be drawn to it. Seems to attract a fair share of drifters comin' through here."

Ty pulled a long smoke from under the flap of his shirt pocket, offering it to C. G. Shean. The man waved it off.

"I'll take a plug now and again," C. G. said gratefully. "I seen that badge under your pocket cover. The sun shined right square on it. I met my share of rangers when I was workin' the trail in New Mexico. You're the only tallgrass ranger they is, I reckon."

C. G. tapped his cane on the floor for added emphasis. Ty scratched a light on his boot heel and lit his black cheroot, enjoying its aroma.

"I'm on loan," Ty admitted, setting his situation straight for the old rancher. "It's high time I wander down and take a look-see at that ravine you mentioned."

"Good idea. Before you do, I'll fetch some grub. The lumbago has slowed me down a touch. It will take just a minute or two for these legs to get moving."

Several moments later, he handed Ty three biscuits, along with a sizeable strip of dried meat. "Venison. This old trail marker's favorite. The water over yonder in the ravine is comin' from a spring. It's fit to drink."

"Much obliged, C. G. It's right nice of you."

The old rancher offered a gnarly hand to Ty and held on awkwardly to Ty's fingers, seemingly making an assessment of Ty as he departed. "If this here thieving rascal were to show his sorry face on this property or come near that corral, I won't hesitate none to shoot him clean through! Bunged up like I am, well, a man sure 'nuff could die out here without no horses."

"I don't question none your line of reasonin'," Ty agreed respectfully. "It wouldn't sit well if I came back with a dead man, though. The marshal, he's determined to have a trial back in Tanglewood. He's got himself rancher problems, since these night-ridin' thieves I've been trackin' stole half the horses 'round them parts. Seems they done the same down in Cherokee territory and then moved up to Kansas. There's a bit of killin', too. Entire remudas been stole time and time again—including mine! Always in the dead of night. We rounded up some of his men in Abilene. There was gunplay, and the marshal and the sheriff was shot.

"Dead?"

"I reckon not. But I can't be sure."

The old man's tired eyes narrowed. There was no fear in them. "I'll be near where my rifle is handy, McCord."

Ty smiled broadly. He was familiar with the determination he saw in C. G. Surviving on the frontier needed that kind of resolve.

Leading Grey, Ty quickly sighted the little trail leading to the ravine. Seldom used and overgrown in spots, it nonetheless would easily be recognized by a seasoned rider. Small trees circled the lowest spot in the ravine.

Saddleless, Grey licked in the glistening water. Busy squirrels scampered up and down trees, and a lone prairie chicken flushed from the waist-high tallgrass. A killdeer darted off to a stump, sending its penetrating cry of disapproval to the new arrivals. Ty's elevated senses took in the early evening's sounds. Finally, the boiling winds had died, which made his low-lying resting place somewhat bearable. He carefully thumbed three new cartridges into his pistol. Leaning against a sturdy cottonwood, he waited patiently for the outlaw who might never appear. His hunch was a direct descendant of experience in the ways of pitiless and lawless men on the run.

Darkness began to settle in. After a short while, there was a faint sound of distant movement on the trail; it could have been anything. Low-flying, dark birds streamed overhead. Closer now, the sound of a spent horse laboring mightily came toward him.

"The man with the bandana! On my stallion!" Ty flexed

the long fingers of his gun hand. His breathing began to slow. In plain sight, the alert rider slid from the palomino, carefully surveying his surroundings. Noticing Grey browsing a short distance away, the rider alertly stepped in the direction of the brute.

"That's as far as you go, feller," Ty demanded calmly.

The thief spun around, crouching low.

"Who says so?" the rider shouted menacingly, while dropping his gun hand to his side.

"Unbuckle that gun belt where you stand! Now! I'll not dicker with a man that steals my remuda," Ty said viciously, stepping out of the shadows.

"No man takes my gun! Some died trying. Least of all, no weak-kneed rancher," the man with the bandana shouted.

"A low-life horse thief such as yourself might just be a touch slow with his draw. That hot wind workin' on your ass all day saps the quickness from a man. You'll be goin' back to Tanglewood in one condition or another. If droppin' that gun belt ain't no option, then make your play!" Ty's command was steady and deliberate.

The unmoving silhouette of the tall ranger stood only a few steps away when Sim's flashing hand snatched his pistol from its holster. In a blinding instant, it was strangely dangling from his hand and slipped from his bloody fingers, clattering among the rocks at his feet. Ty's pinpoint shot had destroyed his elbow.

Prairie Justice

Ten days had passed since the capture of Cole Clifford and Sim Collins. The most famous trial in the tallgrass country was about to take place in the Tanglewood Courthouse. A federal judge would be presiding over the case, set to begin in two days. Juan and Roy seemed unable to stem the conversation surrounding the startling event.

Roy sat comfortably on Ty's front porch. "When things was at their worst, this stranger come right up to me, saying Ty had sent word for help. He even apologized for being late. Fellow named Harper Craig. Before things quieted a bit, he fetched the marshal and the sheriff. They'd done been shot! He was strong as a doggone mule. Picked up that marshal and put him in Mr. Clifford's fancy, dolled-up car, leaving all them big windows and doors wide open. Next, he commenced to flush them passengers out of them boiling-hot cars and set 'em walking back to Abilene. They didn't complain none, neither."

Roy continued on. "Cole Clifford was shot up plenty. Screaming like a stuck hog. Sheriff Goodnight weren't real bad. Just couldn't walk none, so this Craig fella set him down in the shade of a tree opposite an empty horse car. Then me an' Juan threw five of them thievin' devils we captured in the horse car right square in front of the sheriff. That's when I gave the sheriff my scattergun. Later on, we done went to where the three dead thieves was and covered each one with one of Clifford's special-made bed-sheets we found. Three or four thieves escaped. We was shorthanded, you see. I was shot plumb through my calf. That's how come you seen me limping around," Roy said proudly.

Several young boys sat cross-legged, riveted to Roy's tale and sipping Liz's lemonade. "Weren't long at all before Juan come back to the train with another dead man on the back of his horse. It was a snake-faced outlaw wearing them jingle-bob spurs. He weren't shot none, but he was dead enough. Doc Diederich said it was likely a broken rib or two pierced his no-good heart or something. 'Cause he was done bled out! He got what he deserved, alright."

"We didn't see hide nor hair of Ty 'til sunup the next day. All of us participants was in Abilene by then, so's the sheriff could empty his jail of all them drunk drovers. He had to make room for them boys we had in our custody," the old buffalo soldier said, displaying a wide, gap-toothed smile.

"Well, whilst we was enjoying our mornin', here comes Ty on Grey. They was bringing in the ramrod of them night-ridin' raiders. The man's arm was all slinged up where Ty done away with his elbow. Ty said he drew down on him. Seems Ty stayed that night with a man named C. G. Shean, an old trail marker from the early days. Anyways, he borrowed one of Shean's rides. Left his stolen palomino stallion behind, so's he could come return later and bring it back to where it rightly belonged."

Roy waited long enough for the boys to dip out new helpings from the lemonade bucket before he continued on. "Cause of all the goin's on the women folk done delayed that there hoedown they was plannin' 'til after the trial.

"Clifford, he hired two high-fallutin' lawyers from back east somewhere to try and save his no good hide. Ain't no use. The ramrod Ty brung in is betting on the same lawyers. It don't matter none; them we done captured is goin' to testify against 'em both, so's they don't have to pull no hemp. Don't seem logical to old Roy that a jury is about to go against testimony from our tallgrass ranger or the marshal neither. Don't you forget about him. And one more thing, boys. When Ty come back here, Liz was waitin'—and me and Juan, we seen what happened! She laid down the law right here on this porch. There weren't no questions from that tall drink a water, neither."

Readings

The Annals of Kansas, Daniel W. Wilder, 1875

The Beginning of the West, Louise Barry, 1972

The Border Outlaws, J. W. Buel, 1881

The Chisholm Trail, Sam Ridings, 1936

Civil War on the Western Border 1854–1865, Jay Monaghan, 1955

The Cowboy and His Horse, Sydney Fletcher, 1951

Great Gunfighters of the Kansas Cowtowns 1867–1886, Nyle Miller and Joseph Snell, 1963

Historic Kansas, Margaret Whittemore, 1954

Kansas the Priceless Prairie, Mary Engle, 1976

Noted Guerrillas, John N. Edwards, 1877

Quantrill and the Border Wars, William Esley Connelley, 1909

Rebellion in Missouri, Hans Christian Adamson, 1961

The Santa Fe Trail, Robert Luther Duffus, 1930

Sentinel of the Plains, George Walton, 1973

The True Story of Charles W. Quantrell, J. P. Burch, 1923

Wonderful Old Lawrence, Elfriede Fischer Rowe, 1971

CPSIA information can be obtained at www.ICGtesting.com
Printed in the USA
LVOW11s0830291113

363030LV00001B/137/P